Every Eye

Books by Isobel English

The Key That Rusts, a novel (1954)

Every Eye, a novel (1956)

Four Voices, a novel (1961)

Life After All, short stories (1973)

Isobel English

Every Eye

INTRODUCTION BY
Neville Braybrooke

A Black Sparrow Book
DAVID R. GODINE · *Publisher*
BOSTON

This is
A Black Sparrow Book
published in 2006 by
David R. Godine · *Publisher*
Post Office Box 450
Jaffrey, New Hampshire 03452
www.blacksparrowbooks.com

First published in Great Britain in 1956 by
André Deutsch, Ltd., London
This edition published by arrangement with
Persephone Books, Ltd., London

The Black Sparrow Books pressmark is by Julian Waters
www.waterslettering.com

LIBRARY OF CONGRESS CATALOGING-IN-PUBLICATION DATA
English, Isobel, 1920–1994.
Every eye / Isobel English ; introduction by Neville Braybrooke.
p. cm.
"A Black Sparrow book."
ISBN 1-57423-199-5
1. Intergenerational relations—Fiction. 2. Honeymoons—Fiction.
3. Ibiza (Spain)—Fiction. I. Title.
PR6055.N45E95 2006
823'.914—dc22
2006002858

FIRST PRINTING
Printed in the United States of America

TO
MY MOTHER AND FATHER
WITH LOVE

Introduction

When my wife died in 1994, there was a confusion about names in the obituary columns. Some called her by her married name of June Braybrooke, others by that of Isobel English—the pseudonym under which she began to publish in 1954, when she was thirty-four. Then, to make the confusion even worse, there was her maiden name of Jolliffe and her married name of Orr-Ewing, dating back to 1941, when she married Ronald Orr-Ewing.

Stevie Smith knew her as June Braybrooke, although in 1954, when *The Observer* sent her a batch of novels for review that included June's novel *The Key That Rusts*, she had no idea who "Isobel English" was. After the review came out, June invited her to lunch—but signed the letter Isobel English. Stevie, in her reply, pretended that she knew who it was. Only when the Braybrookes opened the front door did she discover the truth.

Present at the meeting, and invited to lunch, was Hugo Manning, whose work I had begun publishing during the war in my little review *The Wind and the Rain*. When we had no money, he would take us out to meals. Sometimes he would copy out poems for June in his elegant, spindly handwriting. She put a line from one of them at the top of a notebook: "Our journey to a far Canaan is always about to begin."

Sometimes friends do extraordinary things. On June's first publication day, he rang at four o'clock in the morning from Reuters, where he worked on the night shift, to announce that he had seen a not very favorable notice of *The Key That Rusts* in the *Daily Telegraph*. "Who is it by?" I asked anxiously. "John Betjeman," came the reply. I had to wait several hours for the newsagents to open up—and by then June had the seeds of a migraine.

Two years later, in 1956, Betjeman turned a complete literary somersault when he reviewed her second novel, *Every Eye*, for the same paper. He declared that the author had "helped to explode the dying myth that the novel is becoming extinct." He quoted two sentences to show the power of the writing. First he chose this, to illustrate how much she was on the mark when describing a travel scene:

> *Now we are swinging through France, down the lighted tracks where all the night long men*

> *in berets and butcher-blue dungarees sweat
> rough wine and oil through their red and open
> pores . . .*

Second he chose this, to reveal her skill in delineating character:

> *At least we had the barren fields of our incompatibility between us, which made us better
> than strangers.*

He also informed his readers that though the novel was short, "none of it can be skipped."

Almost forty years on, this review was to be recalled as "a rapturous notice" by the anonymous obituarist of the *Daily Telegraph*. After I had first read it to June, she said: "I am over the moon." Yet within an hour there was a migraine on the way.

June's third and last novel was *Four Voices*, published in 1961. BBC Television dramatized several scenes, and it was arranged that Robert Kee should interview the author. She grew steadily more nervous as this prospect neared, but Kee tried to put her mind at rest by telling her the day before what his first question would be, so that she could write a reply and pin it to her skirt as a prompt. Nonetheless, on the afternoon when she was due to go to the studio, there were signs of an oncoming migraine, for one learns to detect them: one sign is a muddling of words. During lunch, at which she scarcely pecked, she remarked: "I've got a monkey upside-down in my nose."

When the BBC car drew up outside, she got in with a determined step—and waved: "I hope they won't ask me to witness the Treaty of Utrecht or anything like that." Was this a joke? Or was it indication that an attack was gathering? We smiled and hoped for the best.

Most of her life June was subject to these attacks. Yet there were long spells—even months—when none struck. And then an attack would quickly trigger a row. Booking seats for plays or operas, or accepting dinner invitations, was always chancy. Her doctor in Hampstead, who saw her in the midst of one, said that it was the worst that he had ever seen. His advice to her was to keep on with the writing but to avoid the limelight.

Only twice did she ignore this. In 1974, when she won the Katherine Mansfield Prize for her volume of stories *Life After All*, she decided to go to Menton to accept it. Then, in her final years, she gave two public readings of short stories to help the Henry St.

John Ecumenical Group on the Isle of Wight. On the rare occasions that newspapers rang, she would say, "I'm a very private person," and then hand the receiver to me. For several months in 1974, Kay Dick tried to persuade her to be tape-recorded; eventually June gave in, and the interview, in Kay's book *Friends and Friendships*, is the only one with her ever published. She thought that Kay had a special genius for these things and was an admirer of the interviews that she had recorded with Stevie Smith and Ivy Compton-Burnett. They were included in Kay's book *Ivy and Stevie* (1971), which she dedicated to us. Kay's tape with June ran for two hours.

Stevie, in her review of *The Key That Rusts*—the first novel, which Betjeman had disliked—summed up June's talent in these words: "She has a very sagacious and original voice—a voice of our times, ironical and involved, and yet a peculiar voice." This definition, never bettered, was repeated in both *The Times* and *The Independent* at her death.

The Key That Rusts, when it came out in 1954, went into three impressions. Elizabeth Bowen, who reviewed it, wrote in December to say that she could hardly believe it was a first novel; she also urged June to submit two short stories, which June had sent her, to the *London Magazine*. John Lehmann turned them down, as he did all her work, but a third short story, titled "Feuille Morte," was accepted by the *New Statesman* by return of post. Later, after her third novel appeared, Elizabeth Bowen wrote once more to encourage her to collect a volume of stories, even if, as had been her own experience, it meant including stories that had not already appeared in magazines.

I read this letter when it arrived, but the first letter I did not see until recently, when I discovered it tucked into one of June's notebooks. She had a secretive side to her character, and although we lived in the same house, she often said nothing to me about her literary activities. She did, however, show me a letter she had from the American publishers Little, Brown about her first novel, in which they asked if a happy ending could be added. She simply said no. More significantly, during these early days of her career, came the news that *The Key That Rusts* had been short-listed for the Somerset Maugham Award, tying for first place with Iris Murdoch's first novel, *Under the Net*. In the event, the judges were unable to decide which should be the winner, so the prize was given to the runner-up, Kingsley Amis's *Lucky Jim*.

❖   ❖   ❖

June, who was born on 9 June 1920, died on 30 May 1994. She was the second daughter of John Mayne Jolliffe, whose father had been an impoverished Welsh schoolmaster who, seeking his fortune, had decided to emigrate with his family of fifteen children from the Rhondda Valley to Australia. June, in her thirties, used to dream of writing the libretto for an opera to be called "To the Antipodes." Her father had a powerful voice and sang with much tremulo; he felt, though, that he could never be a star. His second love was sailing—but there again, he felt he could never be a crack helmsman. So he turned to being a businessman, and was to grow disappointed and embittered. He could take petty revenges on life, as when he said to his youngest daughter: "Why don't you make as much money as A. J. Cronin?"

June's mother, May Guesdon, was born in Tasmania in 1879. The family was of Huguenot stock and proud of it. Her grandfather had come from Brest to Hobart, where he settled and ran a fleet of whalers. When her father was widowed and May did not care for his second choice of wife, she and her many younger brothers and sisters moved out to a house on their own, though May was still only in her mid-teens. She was strong-willed, striking, and had Titian hair. At the age of thirty she read Balzac in order to teach herself French, which she spoke in a forceful fashion. After her marriage to John Jolliffe, at the beginning of the twentieth century, they thought that they and their baby daughter Mitty might live in South Africa, but when they reached Cape Town they decided to sail on to England, where they had a number of relations.

Before the First World War, May had had an audition with Nellie Melba when she was in London; she had advised her to go to Paris and take lessons. May never tired of telling people of her reply: "I must explain, Madam, I have a young daughter and a husband, whom I cannot leave." When May became my mother-in-law, I soon realized that she had never forgotten the sacrifice of her talents as a mezzo-soprano. At the Onslow Court Hotel in South Kensington, where she lived for some years as a widow, she would reenact for me scenes from Shakespeare's *Macbeth*—and silence the dining room. In Macbeth's great soliloquies, she would clutch at the fork before her as if it were a dagger.

June described her upbringing to Kay Dick as that of a "very delicate" and "very groggy sort of child." At the age of two, she was found to have a tubercular spine, and her mother rushed her to a convent in Brittany, where she could have saltwater baths at half the price of those in England. She was confined to a wheelchair, and "one terrible year" her tonsils were removed under local anesthetic. The latter left her with a terror of doctors, which never quite disappeared. During the nine months of each year that she spent at St.-Jacut-de-la-Mer, her father, riding a motorbike from Dinard, would arrive for brief stays. In the sports annex he and his wife would give song recitals to the boarders, who were mainly lady boarders.

Then, just as suddenly as June had been rushed over to Brittany, she was whisked back to London. The French doctors pronounced her cured. The plan was that she should now go to a convent boarding school at Burnham-on-Sea. But though only eight, she had a feeling that all was not well at home. To Kay Dick she was more explicit: "My father was getting tied up with somebody." There was an unsettling background of his women friends drifting in and out—one of whom, she used to recall, lived in a flat off "Courtfield Gardens, Earls Court." Early on, June developed a keen memory for place names.

In *Every Eye*, Hatty Latterly, a failed concert pianist, reflects on the melancholy sound of the road called Marloes, which links Earls Court with Kensington High Street. In her late teens, when June went down with quinsy in Belgium, she consoled herself by repeating its beguiling French name—*angine de Vincent*. Ten years before, when her mother told her that her new school was in Somerset, she felt that nothing could go wrong at a place that had "summer" in its name. How mistaken she was! The boarding school, called La Retraite at Burnham-on-Sea, was far from a paradise.

June was not a Catholic and so was not allowed to go to Holy Communion with the other girls. Yet because she had such a good voice, the nuns pressed more and more solos on her at High Mass on Sundays. Some of the professed nuns, she believed, should not have been let loose among children—in particular one math teacher. If the girls in her class misbehaved, they would be forced to stand in a row, open their mouths, and have salt placed on their tongues. Then the order would be given: "Swallow—and offer it up for the persecuted Russians."

During her last term, when she was sixteen, June asked her parents if she might become a Catholic: "I did not have any Church of England upbringing. What sort of religious doctrine I had been taught was Catholic dogma." Her parents refused: her father was not interested in religion, and although her mother never went to any other church than a Catholic one, her loyalty to the Huguenots prevented her from ever taking the step to Rome. June herself did not become a Catholic until a fortnight before our wedding, in December 1953.

When she had first gone to La Retraite, her father had given her a dispatch case with writing paper, envelopes, and stamps. Before she left for Paddington Station, he had promised her: "We'll make a writer of you yet." He was thinking of how badly she joined up her letters. His words, though, were to have a prophetic ring—even if not quite in the way that he intended. When she left La Retraite, he decided he would send her to the St. James Secretarial College, reminding her that a good secretary is a pearl of great price. Momentarily the impact of this decision missed her, because she could only think of the wonders of the pearl—its iridescence and its pellucid beauty.

Later, when she was grown up, she became a collector of jewelry, and believed that it could be mixed, whether it was inherited or bought at Oxfam, or Woolworth's, or Asprey's in Bond Street. When Olivia Manning died in 1980 and left her a legacy, she went out and chose a pair of gold and turquoise earrings. As a child, when she had heard the history teacher talk of the Venerable Bede, she thought at first she meant a necklace.

June survived two terms at the St. James Secretarial College. Then she implored her father to let her study Literature. Finally he caved in, and Kenneth Allott was chosen to be her tutor.

Allott was a rising poet of the thirties. In 1937 he had co-authored, with Stephen Tait, a novel titled *The Rhubarb Tree*, which became famous because the heroine's voice was only heard on the telephone. To June he dictated notes on James Joyce, whose surname she spelled "Choice," and on T. S. Eliot, whose surname she spelled with two l's. In exchange she told him details of the preparations being made for her presentation at Court: "I said how on the night all the famous photographers kept their studios open, so that debs could turn up before or after they had been to Buckingham Palace. The entrances to their studios were banked high with flowers." June Jolliffe was presented on 12 May 1937.

Meanwhile, she and Allott continued to explore *The Waste Land*. In her bedroom she would copy out on slips of paper the foreign lines and leave them for her parents to ponder. At night she would go out and see friends who lived in Soho basements, scraped by on the dole, and drank out of jam pots. Eliot's books in their rainbow-colored covers were regarded as a Bible. June's parents referred to these friends as a *galerie.* On other evenings she would go to dances at Sandhurst, or to balls such as the Beaufort Hunt. At the latter she heard a rider say: "Brute refused the jump. Turned her around. Damned if she didn't do it again."

These memories were to find their way into the many notebooks and diaries that she began keeping in 1950. In a diary of 1938, which survives, there is an account of how she took a job as a cloakroom attendant at Vasco's Hairdressing Salon in the West End. One day proved enough because there were rats in the basement. The head receptionist, over thirty, was "a hard little blonde ... with skin like orange peel." The last phrase was to surface in *Every Eye*, about a French woman who boards the train at Toulouse for Barcelona and whose skin is said to have "the texture of orange peel."

My wife usually wrote her books fully dressed—but lying on a bed. *Every Eye* was the exception, for she went down to the dining room each morning at eleven for two hours: "I lose a sharp edge after that." Never did I read a complete manuscript until it was ready to be professionally typed. Then, after it was returned, June wrapped it in a silk scarf, as was her custom, and delivered it by hand to her publishers—

in this case the firm of André Deutsch. All four of her books were delivered in this manner and the scarves sent back in the stamped, addressed envelopes that she had enclosed. She liked to have a decision on a manuscript within a week and rang up if this was not forthcoming.

A few lines of the novel were drafted in Ibiza, to which we had gone for a belated honeymoon in 1954. On the third page of *Every Eye*, Ibiza is referred to as "the most savage of the Balearic Islands" and, toward the end of the novel, as "the White Island of Nightingales"—a description used by many of the local people whom we met. How savage the island was we were made aware of on our first evening, when we were sitting in the center of Santa Eulalia del Rio and saw an American woman stoned by the villagers because she was wearing trousers. She had to take shelter in the bus in which she had traveled and wait for it to return to the capital of the island.

The novel offers contrasting views of Ibiza: there is that of the picture book, with paths leading off the page to places of serene happiness, and that of blood and sand, where blue-quilled cocks with sharpened beaks and pared claws fight to the death. (Victories are assessed on points—and usually only after each bird is dead. The few tourist agents on the Island in the 1950s kept silent about this.)

Hatty, who comes to Ibiza with a husband con-
siderably younger than herself, has been born with a
squint, which an elderly lover has paid a surgeon to
remove. She learns that "one is born with one's infirmities and . . . must carry them always regardless
of their visible absence." This paradox informs her
life, with the result that she never sees quite dead on.
One is put in mind of E. M. Forster's remark about
the Greek poet Cavafy standing at a slight angle to
the universe. Hatty, too, sees the world at a slight
angle—though, in reality, it may not be Hatty but
the world that is standing at an angle. Inherent in
her attitude to "casting one's bread upon the waters"
is her view that although beggars need our material
support, they owe us something in return: "We must
reach out to the ends of their poor bound stumps
and feel with our bare fingers the true gift of profit
and loss." The sharp-eyed tout of the Pension Termino outside the Barcelona station who picks up
Hatty and Stephen has his own parable to offer on
charity, as he drops a centavo into the upturned hand
of a beggar by the cathedral: *Mieux que je donne
aux pauvres que j'aille a la messe chaque jour.*

In London, Hatty's lecherous uncle Otway is as
much a sinister figure of suspicion as he is a blimp-

ish joke. His new wife, Aunt Cynthia, though once a
friend to Hatty, becomes more and more a cause of
resentment to her as she registers her petty spites.
Hatty's own mother is cast in the role of the Greek
chorus: "Don't go to a man's room alone. Don't give
them your photograph. They will only make a caricature of it . . ." These are some readings that the
novel suggests. Others include a story of oppression
by Hatty's elders, or a story of her late gain of free-
dom by her unexpected marriage to Stephen Latterly.

The working title for the novel had been "The
Path Is Overgrown"—the comment made by the stu-
dent at the end of Act II in Chekhov's *The Cherry
Orchard*. In *Every Eye* the journey from London to
Ibiza is dovetailed with a journey into the past and
the exploration of Hatty's earlier life from her child-
hood until her mid-thirties. Aunt Cynthia had first
told her about the island—and the book opens with
Hatty having just learned of her aunt's death at the
Ipswich County Hospital.

There have been many novels based on the prem-
ise that life is lived forward but understood backward. What distinguished Isobel English's novel from
those of most of her contemporaries was its religious
dimension. Among her writing friends, few had read
the spiritual classics that she had, or had such a

familiar knowledge of the Psalms, and only Stevie
Smith and Muriel Spark had studied the modern
philosopher and mystic Simone Weil, who had died
in 1943. In fact all three had begun reviewing Weil's
books when they began to appear in the 1950s. (In
1950 I had launched Simone Weil, as translated by
Mary McCarthy, in *The Wind and the Rain*: in the
previous year her work had been turned down by
Cyril Connolly for *Horizon* and by some thirty other
literary magazines.) It was this religious dimension
in Isobel English's work that had initially attracted
Antonia White and Graham Greene to her.

Yet she had no sympathy for the term "the Catholic novel," which was much bandied about in the
1950s. Nor was it ever applied to her novels. Reli-
giously speaking she remained a novelist for whom
the Last Words of Jesus had a profound resonance
and carried an illumination with them. Two lines
from the Surrealist artist Ithell Colquhoun, quoted
in the novel, also made an indelible impression:

> *Stretch out your hand in the dark*
> *It will be taken.*

These lines answer in Hatty a predisposition to be
led and represent a statement of faith.

June often repeated them. She believed that

before settling down to work a writer should say: "Let the Light shine through me." She was convinced that the veil between this world and the next was a thin one: those on the other side could be "mobilized," to use a term of which she and her sister were fond. June had notable psychic powers, but was loath to talk about them, although in her short stories, such as the title story in *Life After All*, she writes freely about psychic matters, and, in *Every Eye*, Aunt Cynthia's son Ted, at her funeral, sees an old friend of the family standing by the graveside whom everyone else knows is too bedridden to venture outside. Ted posts Hatty a "spooky" letter in which he records these happenings, so as to give her "the creeps under all that Mediterranean blue."

The strands are all pulled together in the final scene, which takes place on a mountain behind Santa Eulalia del Rio. Here Hatty and Stephen go in search of a fourteenth-century hermit's place of retreat. At first, it appears a gleaming sugarhouse. Then, as they draw closer and enter it, they see it is dominated by a plain wooden cross, with no figure of a Christus with His arms outstretched to enfold the world. This is the dark night of the soul of which mystics and saints have spoken. On the walls are scratched words with signatures and dates. They are petitions. They are also messages to future pilgrims that nothing in life is ever fortuitous. They hold a special meaning for Hatty and Stephen. Here is one of the most powerful passages in the book:

> *Nothing is ever lost that is begun, no word spoken that can ever be broken down to unco-ordinated syllables, no tear shed that will leave only a powdering of white salt. Every-thing must go on, and on, and on, repeating itself and gathering force for the ever that is still only the bright whiteness of eternity med-itated on by mystics and recluses.*

June's first husband, Ronald Orr-Ewing, from whom she was divorced in 1953, she regarded as a mentor. It was appropriate that she should dedicate one of her novels to him and their only daughter, Victoria, who was born in 1942. June and Ronald met early during the war, when they found themselves in the same Kensington boarding house in Campden Hill Gardens. He had intellectual leanings, which, among her family, were regarded as "awfully bad manners." Still, her twenty-first birthday was fast approaching, and then she could and would marry whom she pleased. Not long after their marriage, Ronald was called up into the Air Force—though he refused a commission. Auden was one of his chosen poets in whose work in the 1940s he tried to interest his father-in-law, but without success. He was much more sympathetically in tune with his mother-in-law, who knew reams of Shakespeare by heart, could recite from Balzac and Browning, and decided at the age of eighty to revisit Australia, choosing to travel on a cargo boat.

Ronald was an inspired teacher, although Stevie Smith thought that "sage" would be a better term. At the Aliens' Office and at Scotland Yard, where he was in charge of the Crime Prevention Committee, he attracted many friends. He was ahead of his time, and observed how suddenly the police establishment switched from being in favor of capital punishment to being against it. He also produced a revolutionary White Paper on Prison Reform, and his opening words, on arriving at Parkhurst Jail, have become part of prison lore: "I've come to let the buggers out." His final years were spent as an antique dealer, mainly in Hebden Bridge, Yorkshire, where he was to die in 1988.

He was always seeking talent to promote. Many students he set on their way to high positions in the academic world, and many artists owe their first exhibitions to his patronage. In his early years with June, he told me, she often astonished him with her comments: "Everything taken out of context can be a deception"; "I like Rider Haggard, but can't stand Jane Austen"; "Only our intelligence will save us." In 1950, when she began to draft short stories, he could not have been more enthusiastic. "Encouragement is all important when one is beginning to write," she said. Later, when she said she wanted to start a novel, his admiration knew no bounds. His advice was simple and practical: "Go out and buy a notebook." When it was filled, he said: "Buy another . . ." That was how *The Key That Rusts* came into being. During its progress, he would comment: "You have passion and style, and compose like a great artist." In *Every Eye*, Ted, who is partly based on Ronald, offers a variation on these words to Hatty.

June never failed to show Ronald her books in manuscript. Apart from myself, there were only four others whom she treated in this way: Francis King, his sister Elizabeth, Elizabeth's husband John Rosenberg, and Muriel Spark. Muriel chose the titles for June's second and third novels, and in her autobiography, *Curriculum Vitae* (1992), she declared: "June wrote exquisite novels under the name of Isobel English."

Introduction

On June's birthday in 1952, when she was thirty-two, Ronald gave her the *Collected Stories of Katherine Mansfield*, edited by John Middleton Murry. It was in this book that she tried out the pseudonym of Isobel English—"but in pencil," as she informed the audience at Menton that had gathered to see her receive the Katherine Mansfield Prize. She told them, too, that in her house she had Katherine's sofa, which had been left to her by Anne Estelle Rice, whose portrait of Katherine Mansfield now hangs in the National Gallery of New Zealand. Lying on it, Katherine had said to Anne after a dreadful attack of coughing: "It's a queer world, darling, but in spite of everything, it's a rare, rare joy to be alive."

On 1 April 1994, June was diagnosed as having leukemia. Until three days earlier, she had been working on our life of Olivia Manning, which was a joint enterprise. Another four days later she was a patient in the Royal Free Hospital in Hampstead and her condition was serious. Sometimes there would be an improvement, but it was never sustained. In May, in her last month, a group of doctors asked her, on their round of the ward, what she saw from the window. "A dim light," she said, "but there is hope in the clouds." In our bedroom at home, among her special books, were Proust, Edward Upward, Katherine Mansfield, Denton Welch, Ivy Litvinov, Forster, David Gascoyne, St. Theresa of Avila, and a well-thumbed copy of the fourteenth-century *Cloud of Unknowing,* by an unknown mystic. She had him in mind when she wrote the last pages of *Every Eye.* On another favorite shelf she had the works of Ezra Pound and D. H. Lawrence.

Each morning at home when the parcel post arrived, she would shout to me: "What has the old *Sunday Telegraph* sent you?" One day as I undid their parcel, I shouted up from the hall: "They've sent *The Letters of Lawrence,* Volume Four."

"Can I have a sneak preview?" she asked.

An hour later she called down: "Come up immediately. I've found something for ever."

I raced up the stairs.

"Listen," she said as I entered our bedroom: "Lawrence was traveling and didn't know of Katherine Mansfield's death until about three weeks later. Here is what he wrote to Murry: 'The dead don't die. They look on and help.'"

That was what we had put on June's memorial card.

NEVILLE BRAYBROOKE
Isle of Wight, 2000

Every eye must weep alone
Till I Will be overthrown.
                    —W. H. AUDEN

Every Eye

I heard today that Cynthia died last Friday afternoon at the Ipswich County Hospital, just after a cup of tea.

This news has affected me in a way that I did not expect. One minute I was all set with my resentments close-knit and compressed, and the next it was as if a great wave had suddenly crashed shoreward, under-cutting and breaking into the very foundations of my own life.

So that is what a death is like—to the people who harbor dislikes. The mysterious disappearance in-volves them as well, and they are left uneasy with a new set of problems to grapple with. . . .

. . . It is six years since I last saw Cynthia, six years since I cut myself free from the inquisitive disap-proval; the light unfriendly laugh that always accom-panied her sharpest barbs—the honey and the gall mixed to such a smooth consistency that they were inseparable. And yet I should have known the reason for this; I am always talking about a true sense of vocation—the time when I was going to become a pianist, and now once more when I am trying to put together the bits and pieces of my life to start off with a husband who is so many years younger than I.

Cynthia married my uncle nineteen years ago, and from that moment the disciplines of her vocation were applied. I had watched the efforts of day-to-day living drag the tendrils of flyaway hair into an iron-gray cap, the wet forget-me-not blue eyes sink into their bruised hollows to become the color of stones. The last time I saw her, the most noticeable features were the blunted spades of teeth and the sharp incisors flanking them; these were primitive and vestigial weapons of defense, as if they were the sole means by which she could survive.

"Imagine being able to dedicate one's life to a single person." Stephen, my husband, is still young enough to be able to speak in this way. "It's like a talent; it makes up for religion," he had said. Cynthia was heroic in her selflessness. To eke out the small disability pension of her husband she had gone quietly to work in other people's houses at the rate of two-and-six pence an hour; and I was not able to support this degree of heroism and what it did to her.

It is strange that this news should arrive today, the eve of our departure. Tomorrow morning Stephen

and I are to set off for Ibiza, the most savage of the
Balearic Islands. We have been married a year and
this is a long-promised holiday. Now it seems something over and above, an involuntary, almost predes-
tined, mark of respect to a dead person, for it was
Cynthia who first told me of this place when I first
met her, about the time of my fourteenth birthday.

It was a Sunday in late August, summer over for me
after the return from a bleak two weeks by the sea in
the company of rich school friends and their well-
meaning parents. These people had regarded nakedness at the sea's edge as a kind of medicinal purge, a
self-conscious conceit that was as repulsive for me
to observe as to take part in. In damp misery I had
huddled beneath the short wrap, conscious of my
thin arms and flat chest, while the other children
bounded about unselfconsciously in the white
bathing dresses that they so adequately filled; their
legs and arms were the color of light beechwood in
spite of the absence of the sun behind the tight gray
sky. I longed for the brilliant camouflage of my cre-
tonne dresses; this material used principally for the
making of chair covers lasted forever, my mother
said. One could never sit it out. Sometimes in the past
I had questioned the boldness of pattern and design,

comparing it unfavorably to the fine sprigged cottons of other children's dresses; now on the hard flint beach at Selsey, I longed for all the wild disorder of enormous moss roses and gladioli. I thought with nostalgia of home and the security of proper covering—the musty smell of the upright piano with its beautiful faded pink silk behind the latticed fretwork.

Once it was over, the sting went away quickly. I could think with detachment of those purple rubbery people and their smell of grown-up and wet wool, leaping about on the windy beach, shouting in wild fulfillment when they stayed the course of a quoit in their pale clenched fists. They became like the wax fairy dolls on the top of other people's Christmas trees who could only draw feelings of envy and inadequacy by their presence; all the rest of the year they were hidden away, covered in black paper. My friends' parents were really quite presentable in their winter overcoats.

Cynthia had walked up the front steps of our ground-floor flat that Sunday afternoon, on the arm of my handsome Uncle Otway. I saw them through the net curtains. I had been practicing the piano in the sitting room and I heard the scrape of their shoes on the stone. I waited for the tap on the glass pane, for he would never bother to summon us with the bell.

When it came I rushed to the top of the back stairs and cried down into the black, closed-in hole: "Mum, it's Uncle Ot and someone I've never seen before."

My mother opened the kitchen door and let out the light, "Can't *you* go to the door?" Her hands were covered with flour. "I don't know why you're so peculiar about the door when he comes. Your poor father's brother. I don't know what you think we would have done without him."

I turned away; I knew that I would have to answer the door now. Already they were tapping on the wood and flipping at the letterbox.

The strange woman was very small. Coming into the hall in front of my uncle she barely came level with his shoulder. She wore a light gauzy dress tied at the waist by a velvet sash; her eyes were the brightest china blue I had ever seen—apart from those of Puff, our white cat.

"So you are Hatty." She mouthed the words carefully, like our dressmaker when her mouth was full of pins. Later I was to discover that this deliberate care to sharpen the vowel sounds just prevented the broadness that would have been so much more pleasing to every ear but her own. At the time I thought that she was so small and pretty that I admired even

5

this; it seemed to typify her elegance, as did the thin pointed shoes she wore.

My Uncle Otway reminded me of a big brown bear in his hairy tweed coat. He flapped his arms around her shoulders; he was her background.

"I met this sweet person last year when I was in Barcelona. She's a native of one of the islands, Ibiza—or do you call it Ibeetha, darling?"

I did not know what they were talking about; once in Barker's teashop I had heard a woman singing to the violin, "Oh! Follow the Big Corona, that comes all the way from Barcelona." But the island's name simply sank like a stone into my mind.

Cynthia had looked round the L-shaped sitting room; at the white-painted play cupboard; at the unmounted skin of a tiger that my father had shot in India (you could actually see the bullet holes); then her eyes came to rest on the open piano with its upright stand that held the piece of music which I had just been practicing.

"Your Uncle Otway tells me that you play the piano very well," she had said, and at the back of her smile and simple words I could hear the deep billowing voice of Uncle, explaining away my small successes in the Royal Academy exams; my aspiration; my father's death; my mother's struggle for our survival; and how good it would be if I could be "persuaded, not forced, mind you, because I believe in people having a will of their own," into going to one of those secretarial colleges that overlooked the saddest part of the Park, where the August sheep in their long matted coats bunched together on the balding grass made one long for the cold winds that would drive everyone back to London and bring about the sameness that united those who had been away with the less fortunate who had never left.

"Yes, I do play," I answered, "but I'm only at the beginning." As I spoke I was drawn like a magnet toward the piano stool.

"Do play something for me." Her request seemed exactly to synchronize with the fluttering of the thin music sheets as I felt my way through the pile.

"This is an Arabesque of Debussy," I said as I stood the piece in front of me.

There was a hush—respect and curiosity mingled. She sank into one of the deep armchairs at the other end of the room, beyond the range of my sight. Uncle Otway came toward me, his face creased into smiling lines, just as he had been when we had had our "little talk": "I'll turn for you," he had said, as if we were conspirators.

There was nothing I could do but begin. The

opening bars were clear and uncluttered; I let the running legato of broken chords follow each other from hand to hand. There was no need to worry even when the right hand set up a counter-rhythm to the left; alone I could play it faultlessly. I had to keep the singing line uppermost in my head and let the watery greenness envelop me and create the hard pure tone that would shut me away safely from the cloudy grip of interfering relations, the punctuated footfalls from the flat above, and the acid smells of vinegar and cabbage that wafted down the stairs into our rooms about this time every evening.

I was conscious of heavy breathing at my neck; as I neared the last few bars on the page, a thickly furred hand shot out and swept it over. I had not counted on the violence of this intrusion, I struck a wrong note in a chord, and it went through my head like a gunshot. I did not stop but quickened the tempo in an effort to distract from the mistake. Then I started the slow measured movement that was a rest and respite after the swift flow of the previous passages. The breathing behind me was very close, almost it seemed to disturb and ruffle the short tufts of hair on the nape of my neck; it was nearing the time for the brown paw to strike again. In agitation I turned very slightly, hoping to indicate to Uncle Ot that I could manage on my own. He stood fast, and I saw in that second his eyes crinkle into a concerned smile.

Then I lost my place.

My hands stumbled about incoherently like strangers who had never before touched a keyboard; terrible sounds broke loose, of the kind that tiny children call Chinese music when they strive to express themselves by sheer persistence and force, sometimes by chance bringing together a natural harmony, a beautiful mad sound that can never be repeated. I felt the blood draining away from my face and a still coldness settle round my temples: "I can't go on," I cried at last, "I can't find my place, I don't know what's the matter with me. . . ."

Then my mother came briskly into the room. She looked toward me with annoyance as I sat sniveling on the piano stool; she had obviously been standing outside the sitting-room door and had not liked what she heard. "That's enough," she had said. "Now go and wash your face in cold water."

When I returned to the room a few minutes later, my uncle Otway was sitting at the piano. His eyes were closed, and he played by ear the same Arabesque. Excessive pedaling blurred the edges, his tempo was extravagantly *rubato*, and he struck whole clumps of wrong notes; yet he persevered without perhaps either knowledge or care, swaying from side to side, feeling his way like a blind man through the piece—showing the children how the grown-ups can do it ("and it's not as if I wasn't fond of music myself," he had said at the time of our "little talk"). He came to the last chord; then, taking his foot off the loud pedal, he rose and, putting both hands to his temples, bowed a Hindustani salaam. Cynthia jumped excitedly from her chair and clapped together her little ringed hands. That was the first breath of resentment.

Yet small lacerations heal quickly when one is only fourteen years old; little more than the shallow warmth of a smile, or the quick concentration of an adult eye, can knit together the tiny hurts of the so recent past. Cynthia turned to me now, with all her little white teeth and dimples alive in her face: "You're a great reader, Hatty, I can see that." She looked delightedly at the deep shelves of books, as if she had made a very special discovery; her eyes fell on the encyclopedias and bound copies of *Punch* that my father had left me; she began very cautiously to build me up in my own esteem again. "I've got quite a collection of books, too," she had said. "Nothing like these, of course, but I'd like you to come round one day and have a good browse. Some of the books I've kept since I was a little girl. I still read them. What kind of books do you like best?"

Still cautious but placated almost completely, I answered, a little gruffly I remember: "I like *good* books," and then to illustrate the extent of my knowledge: "I like Rider Haggard very much, but I can't stand Jane Austen."

Six-thirty A.M. and Victoria Station. Stephen's mother, Amy, is already on the platform waiting to see us off; she has brought with her the young girl she hoped that Stephen would marry before he met me. They are dressed almost exactly alike in biscuit-colored shantung and large coolie hats woven with metal thread. I do not really understand this relationship at all, and imagine that they console each other for the loss they have both sustained through me.

Together, Amy and June have packed all the food for our journey; a whole boned chicken and a sirloin of beef concentrated into the depth and width of a two-pound box of sugar; "And, there is a bottle of wine too, my children." Amy is exuberant, her large pale eyes are only just dry; she looks directly into my face as if she is willing me to say something that will unite us all in this great effort to give her son a really good holiday. I feel gloomy and ashen; my conventional thanks are inadequate, I know; but in order to become their accomplices I should have to recast my whole relationship with Stephen and see him only as the happy laughing boy whose snapshot on the sands at Le Zoute remains forever imprisoned behind her eyes.

Stephen flaps in and out of the carriage, his large white hands going like clipped wings. Always at these meetings he is on his guard, watching with a hawk's eye for the outlandish remark that could materialize like ectoplasm from either his mother or his wife. He is a tough ringmaster who keeps us all bucking and prancing right up to the moment of the final whistle blast.

The last few minutes are protracted and uncomfortable. Conversation between people who have not the least idea of each other's whereabouts.

"I love your dress," I say to June faintly. I mean what I say in that I really do appreciate the texture and cut of the pale silk, but she interprets only the shadows of doubtful resentment in my voice. I am, from her point of view, the *daughter-in-law*. "Aunt Amy brought the stuff back from China—ages ago. It is sweet, isn't it?"

"Look after yourselves. It won't be long till we all

meet again. Be sure to write when you get to Paris."
Amy is willing us away now to speed our return;
already she has built a calendar of weeks in her mind
and she wishes to apply the first imaginary stroke
today.

"Post the letters, Mama; don't forget the one for
the bank. Look after yourselves."

At last we are off. Together we lean out of the
carriage window. White emblems of peace fluttering
from the receding platform as well as from the moving train.

An empty carriage, full of light now; trails of
Amy's Fleurs de Rocaille still about us. With curios-
ity we undo the parcels of food. By the time we reach
Newhaven, half of it has gone.

It is strange to find the third-class layer of the
channel steamer made over in chintz upholstery. The
restrooms for men and women are separate. Comfortable sofas and bunks line the walls of the women's
part; a white-starched stewardess bustles behind the
tower of empty enamel basins. There are one or two
figures already prostrate on the bunks; eyes closed,
jaw clenched, painfully unaware of the smooth sweep
of the water, waiting in anguish for the anchor to
drop.

Until we reach Rouen, the Normandy countryside seems only an extension of the Sussex meadows. Stunted and wind-bitten cider apple trees have never been affected by the arm of the sea that has reclaimed the land between them.

To begin with, we are a carriageful of nondescript putty-colored figures. But with the thinning out from station to station, there develop before our accustomed eyes brilliant colored designs on women's dresses, cyclamen gashes on mouths and headscarves, the cerulean of the sky greased and shining on the eyelids of the girl in front of me.

A young Frenchman and his talkative American mother watch from their corner for a sign of a conversational opening. The man sitting next to me is a Central European; when our passports are examined he pats his own on the cover to draw attention to its British blue and gold. "Gilbert's the name," he says smiling, "Gilbert the Filbert, the Knut with a K."

I remember this song from when I was three years old; I wonder whose side he imagines we think that he must have been on. There is a kind of lisping audacity about this man, of the sort that one sometimes comes across in visitors to foreign seaside resorts; a thick-skinned *bonhomie* that aspires to knit together all British holidaymakers as "We Chaps." His strength is in a way his blindness; he does not concern himself with the clever monkeyish habits of the reserved English. "Yes," they will agree to his suggestions, and "Right you are," when they are drawn into an impromptu game of cricket on the beach; yet all the time they will be sustaining an implacable unfriendliness whose victory lies in the continued obtuseness of the person against whom it is directed.

Now the fields open up into short-cropped grassy plains; the trees are higher, elegant weeping branches at the broad river's edge. Everything is flat and exposed. No sheltering hollows in which to take cover during a storm.

Why is it that so many topics of conversation are exhausted in a railway carriage? Perhaps it is that to some it is the only audience that they will ever trap. The time is so short in which to complete the final impression, the space so limited, and the rearing up of the cement platform that will end communication so certain.

Gilbert has begun to explain to us about the business that takes him to Paris en route for Vienna: "There my wife will join me for a holiday, and we will listen to music together." There is a warm Germanic quality in this explanation that completely wipes away all previous English affectations. The mountains, and the garlanded boats on the beautiful river that I have never seen, come suddenly into perspective—this melancholy German romanticism that can never be adequately translated, only transformed into a faded likeness.

The American mother and her son break in, eulogizing over the wonderful cheapness of detergents in England compared with the prices in Paris. Suddenly we are loaded with tips and directions: how not to be done, where to eat cheaply. The young man is so insistent that we feel compelled to follow his instructions or commit treason.

The outer edges of Paris are as frayed and dingy as the suburbs of any great Western capital. We could easily be approaching Euston or King's Cross. This is the first sight of Paris for me, and I look out for similarities to something I already know, some point of contact to set going a chain of background feelings. For Stephen it is different. He can tell the progress of the train with his eyes closed, from his sense of smell alone, it would seem: "Gasworks, Hatty," he says sleepily; "Stinking tunnel"; then "Fresh breeze over the waters of a reservoir." I envy him for his previous knowledge of this city I have never seen. Soon the platform of the Gare St.-Lazare rolls along side of us and we are smiling and saying hopeful farewells to the people who perhaps will never cross our path again.

We have booked no room for the night. "The thing to do," Stephen has said, "is to ring up from the station, or else wander about and try our luck."

I cannot quite bring myself at this stage to the uncertainty of the unknown streets, so we make for a nest of telephone booths. "It's better," I say from the advantage of my extra years, "at least to have some idea of where one is going before we leave the station."

I am suddenly appalled by the detached guttural tones at the other end of the line that announce *"Pas de chambres."* I am about to say something, some kind of word that will soften the precision of those three sharp blows, but there is a crash as the receiver is pushed down onto its distant cradle.

Only in imagination is it rewarding to play on the theme of being stranded in a strange foreign city; then it is delightful, painless, and fraught with thickly jeweled possibilities. Today it is quite different. We are burdened with two pieces of luggage and a shopping bag; the string handle cuts into the skin of my bare wrist, impedes the imagination, weighs me down.

We go down into the Metro. Long drafty tunnels, too near the surface for the controlled silence of air pumps. The carriages rattle in, swinging wildly from side to side of the narrow gauge. There is curly Edwardian scrollwork round the doors; the seats are harsh and austere, like the yellow slatted seats of a station wagon. I sit down on one of the few empty seats and wonder why there are still people foolish enough to stand. Then I see above the window a large notice that reserves the seat I am occupying for the *mutilés de guerre*. It is impossible now to get to my feet with the train swinging so violently and without the use of my hands.

At St.-Germain-des-Prés we come out into the summer light. I am preparing in my mind the approach I shall make to the future hotel proprietor. I have known French so well in the past that now, with the clouding of years and the lack of use, it has become a myth. I think of a thousand phonetic sounds, but no words come to my mind.

Before we go finally into a black entrance that announces Hôtel du Rive Gauche over its doorway, I vacillate. "It's sinister, Stephen—we can't go into the pitch black—it looks like a brothel."

He trundles me firmly through the door. "All these hotels are much the same and this looks reasonable enough."

I feel like letting the bag fall and making for the light again.

Yet once inside, on the black pool of linoleum, there is a soft grayness that seeps down from the upper floors; it is more a degree of darkness than of light, but it makes visible a flight of thick stone stairs and a twisting iron balustrade. There is a bell push on the wall on which is clearly printed the word "Bureau."

A small room on the first floor. *La seule qui reste.* This hotel proprietor has a keen enough sensibility to know that it is not to her advantage to give me a choice.

Dark red wallpaper sprouting with pearly marguerites disguises the partition that cuts off an extremity of what must once have been the drawing room of the house: the fine molding on the ceiling stops dead at the face of one wall. A coarsely carved gilt looking glass reflects the low-sprung divan with its Eastern wool bedspread. There is running cold water from a tap in the corner, and when we have soaked our feet, we uncork the warm emulsified Bordeaux. Now that we have no weight to bear, we can play a game of possibilities, with the evening ahead. "Where shall we eat—we might almost move on— find something better. . . ."

Up until now, the word "Paris" has evoked for me always the end of a mysterious night journey, away from the fishing village in the Morbihan in which I spent most of my childhood; there I imagined the chestnuts must surely be heavier with flowers than any in Bushy Park, the limes in Maytime scenting the avenues would scatter their pale winged fruits around the feet of the young men and women hurrying to their glittering white office buildings; there they would carry on a white high-voltaged existence of wage earning that I have never been able to equate to the duller mole-burrowing efforts of office workers who live in the furnished rooms of Earls Court or Bayswater.

Now that it comes to the reality with both feet on the stone pavement of the boulevard St.-Michel, and later blown by gusts of summery wind through the Luxembourg Gardens, how far are we in reality from the Chelsea Embankment, and do not great cities hold to each other from the core or placenta of all people who live and work in man-made houses?

Stephen takes me to a restaurant on the Seine. It is candlelit with checked cloths, the end of the room built into secluded arbors for those who shun exposure. The main body of the clientele sit in a double row down the center of the room: the silent, the tentative, the unrequited in love, and those who merely wait in their tired knowledge for the fruit to drop into

their laps. Everyone is in some kind of disguise, however flimsy; there are the young who strive to be old
and knowing, the middle-aged with their more deadly
weapon of self-knowledge and self-sufficiency, and
the elderly with all the appearances of infants in their
reckless pursuit of immortality.

Stephen and I are shepherded by a harassed
waiter to a table in the very middle of the room; we
share it with a beautiful-looking couple. The woman's
face has the texture of the finest suede dusted with a
purple bloom, and her hair is spun silver beneath a
crest of white aigrettes. I feel the need to look into
my glass; I wish suddenly that I were not so sallow of
complexion, or my hair the dull brown that it is.

"Don't turn round now," Stephen says suddenly,
"but I think our friend Gilbert is coming into the
restaurant."

To a far table, reserved and respectfully awaited,
not hidden from us on account of our central position, Gilbert of the railway carriage walks, and on
his heels there follows a girl with all the sweet stoop-
ing elegance of her eighteen or nineteen years. As
she passes into the secrecy of the arbor-table, I have
a close view of the Japanese slanting eyes in the white
scented face, the pointed nose with its fine curved
nostrils; heavily outlined below it, the sulky mouth

is locked now over the little teeth that could bite so deep. Gilbert's eyes look straight at us as he walks, manipulating his big body through the matchwood of tables. We watch him through the forest of wine bottles and stalks of mimosa. He thinks for an instant as he turns, and offers to us the thought of what he will buy for his wife tomorrow. I hear again the sound of sighing violins and paddle steamers on the Danube.

When I was seventeen years old, it was definitely accepted by my family that I had a squint. Up until then I had been cajoled and bullied about my "lazy eye"; I had worn corrective glasses and sometimes even a black patch over my good eye. I remember my mother saying to me with conscientious exasperation: "Now that you *have* this deformity, you must think about it more seriously. You will probably have to have the operation." That was the ultimate threat. The eye removed from its socket, I had been told, and laid like an oyster on the senseless cheek, while the surgeon, with tiny sharp forceps and probes, set about tightening the network of muscles that bound it at the back. It was too horrible to contemplate. It was also very expensive. I did not find it too difficult to persuade my mother that I might very well over-come it myself with the help of a book of exercises;

that people with far more obvious disabilities had tried and succeeded with this system. My face was not my fortune, I assured myself, and from the distance of the concert platform no one would notice my cast.

By the time I was eighteen I had almost forgotten the disability; only when I was confronted with a photograph of myself would I register the shock of this plain face whose right eye turned so fatalistically toward the blind wall of a sharp nose.

My eyes are quite straight now, and there is no weakness in the controlling muscles of my right one—yet this has not altered my vision. I am as aware of my corrected squint as if a limb had been removed, leaving only a network of attenuated sensations. I have never been able to give up wearing large-brimmed hats; until lately, I did not go out at night without the protection of smoked glasses.

Stephen knows all these things, which he regards in his benevolence as picturesque.

"You are extraordinary," he says to me when I feel in my purse for my spectacle case, explaining that I am distressed and unnerved at the discovery of Gilbert and his lady friend. "I don't believe you ever see anything dead on, only at a peculiar angle through the corner of your eye."

He does not know how near the truth he is at that

moment, nor realize that one is born with one's infirmities and that one must carry them always regardless of their visible absence.

I don't know what it is that gives to a day the quality of uplift and exaltation. It is perhaps to do with color or wind or sound that penetrates and stirs the brown depths of the imagination and clears it for receptiveness. We awoke this morning, and the tone was gray; deep somnolent gray, beginning with the closed shutters on the house opposite that we can almost lean out of our window and touch. That should have given something, that feeling of distance overcome, but the grayness had got into us even before we set foot outside; all the time I was thinking of the obstructive nearness of things. The muscular effort to propel one leg in front of the other was enormous, the street sounds were grating and one-toned; the same that by yellow sunlight could be lifted to running cadenzas, the accompaniment of winged feet.

We are unlucky over the reservations on the train for Barcelona tonight, and we must take our chance half an hour before the train leaves. Coming out into the prison-yard precincts of the Austerlitz we find it is no place to linger in, have a drink or a cup of coffee; one must hurry away and return at the appointed hour of departure. This place seems only to gain significance for those who are certain to leave it.

Back at St.-Germain-des-Près, in the rue des Saintes-Pères, I feel a homing instinct. Walking toward the hotel we recognize several faces that we have seen the night before. That is the beginning of rehabilitation. We go easily and unspecifically to a restaurant for lunch; it is better and less contrived than the one last night. Already the wariness and stiffness is going out of us, the roll of franc notes depletes itself without our conscious anguish; we are quicker on the 15 percent service.

Quite soon the day is over, and we have fashioned it from its gray beginning into something iridescent and unique.

"I'm glad it wasn't easy going when we started off," I say to Stephen as we drive away from the hotel in a taxi for the Austerlitz once more.

It was exactly five days before my twentieth birthday that Cynthia married my uncle Otway. Everything was very much concealed right up to the last moment.

My mother said to me, after breakfast that Friday morning, "You'd better have a new hat," and before I had time to argue that if she meant it for a birthday present I would rather have a gilt snake necklace, she swept me out of the house in front of her with all the purpose of her strong will driving me up the Earls Court Road toward Kensington High Street.

In the hat department, as she knocked hats on and off my head like ninepins with "too young," "too old," and ruffled my hair into unbecoming puffs over my forehead, she announced suddenly, "Your uncle is marrying Miller. He wishes us to be present tomorrow morning in Marloes Road at eleven-thirty."

I wished that my reactions had been clear. At the time I remember only the thick clouding of perplexity as to who this Miller my mother referred to might be, and *why* she should have been so austerely named. The sound of those melancholy words, Miller and Marloes. I have always been a prey to the hidden qualities of color and scent set going by the impact of sounds. I was enveloped then by the ox-blood brick and the acid and gritty quality of this canal of a road, the workhouse-*cum*-hospital with its dank gardens, and the ancient mulberry trees that shed their black fruit onto the concrete paths like squashed insects, to be dried up by the sun.

"*Cynthia* Miller, of course," my mother was hissing into my ear. "Do try and keep your mouth closed, breathe through your nose. It isn't as if you still had adenoids."

26

I did not then notice her irritation toward me. I had still been unraveling the mystery Miller, and now she had given me the answer.

"Oh, Mum," I cried so that the shop assistant moved away discreetly to be out of earshot, "you sound as if you don't like Cynthia. I think she's sweet. She's going to give me a Victorian bracelet for my birthday."

"No one has mentioned anything about likes or dislikes," my mother had snapped back. "If you choose to be won over by bribes, that is one thing. As for what is suitable, that is quite another. There are some people in this world who do not know the ropes." And from there my mind, in the gray-felted stillness of this hat department, with the distant sunlight filtering through the netted windows, had been suddenly flooded with vaguely nautical feelings. A certain release, like a ray of ease and lightness, came into the whole proceedings, so that my mother and I were no longer even slightly in opposition but united into an ecstatic front.

We chose a round-brimmed sailor hat with a black band flying away into two tails at the back, which, the assistant explained, could be easily unstitched and a wreath of cornflowers or poppies substituted to make it into quite another hat.

At the Registry Office I had stood slightly behind Cynthia, a token bridesmaid in my green taffeta and bronze sandals. My mother and a friend of Cynthia's were the two witnesses, and all through the short ceremony I could hear her breathing through her thinly cut nostrils like an impatient thoroughbred.

Cynthia wore a tight red dress that broke into a mass of pleats just below the hips; her fine silky hair she had gathered into a black chenille snood. She wore no flowers; my uncle had forgotten to order them, she explained outside on the steps; but they were laughing over his forgetfulness as they drove away in the waiting taxi immediately afterward.

When she appeared in our sitting room half an hour later, there were three gardenias pinned to her shoulder.

"Rather putting the cart before the horse, Cynthia dear." My mother had touched her forehead with unmoving lips. I knew that later she would remark on the vulgarity of her pillar-box dress.

"You'll be the next, won't she, Isobel?" Cynthia, since the acquisition of my father's name, had gained stature in her own eyes; I had never before heard her address my mother by her Christian name. Sensible of the narrowing of my mother's eyes, had I not been the subject of this uncomfortable forecast,

I should have allowed the prefix "Aunt" to slip off my tongue. As it was I shut my eyes quickly, then I heard my mother say, "Hatty will marry when the time comes"—as though by incanting such a commonplace she had added sorcery to good breeding.

My time had nowhere at any given point begun. I had merely left school for the Royal Academy of Music, altered the parting of my hair, and acquired the possession of a latch key. No fresh horizons were open to me beyond the shallow confinement of my own white-painted bedroom and the security of my mother's sitting room that now housed the only visible change, a grand piano.

"When we get back," Cynthia continued, "we'll have some gay old times all together. Ted will bring round some of his friends from the Poly."

I experienced a certain mounting excitement at the strange prospect of close contact with members of the opposite sex who were not my relations; the dark serge scissor legs, and the almost human expression of the hard blocked toe-caps of their shoes. Ted was Cynthia's son by the deceased Mr. Miller. He was very small and did not believe in personal hygiene, or laying down his life for his fellow men. He was six weeks older than I—and our meetings had not been encouraged, either by my mother or, for that matter, by Ted himself. He was not present at the wedding that day because it was against his principles to condone something so bourgeoise.

"It would be nice," my mother pushed on, "if Hatty could get to know a few nice young men from the university."

Cynthia was not, on her wedding day, going to allow this to pass. "My Ted has got a whole gang of pals at King's and the L. S. E., so we'll be able to make up quite a party, with two undergrads to a girl, eh, Hatty?"

There was a white cake that Cynthia had made herself. It had a lumpy roughcast surface like the walls of a new bungalow; the top was thickly planted with silver balls that melted in the mouth from the hard shells of mercury to a soft peppermint center. I wanted very much to take away and keep in my souvenir drawer the two white doves on coiled wire springs that she had fixed to a sprig of evergreen in the middle of the cake. It was something to do with being young and old at the same time; marriage and independence were within my physical range, but I was nowhere within their orbit.

When they left for their honeymoon, a taxi at the door to take them to the station and from there by train and boat to "a tiny island, Hatty dear, the third smallest of the Balearics," I wept without restraint; for the passing of time; for the end of one cycle and the beginning of another. Nothing could ever be the same again.

My mother stood on the front steps prodding me in the shoulder blades. "I don't know why you're so upset," she said. "Anyone would think it was a hearse she was driving off in. You needn't worry. They'll be back before the end of the month, and then you'll have a whole lifetime to get sick of her in."

In the pitch-black train at the Austerlitz, we find two window seats; dark strong-smelling leatherette, the floor still damp from the cleaners' rags, and above us the steel slats of the luggage rack.

There must be a great emptying of the mind when one is about to start on a long journey. It is no good clinging to the shreds of last night's anxiety, nor to its comforts; everything must be fresh and completely hard at the edges to withstand the future movement and buffeting.

Soon there are four of us committed to each other in the carriage, and when at last the train draws out of the station and the lights go up, shut in and further marooned by the streaming rain on the windows, through a haze of finely curling tobacco smoke, we take stock of each other.

A dark-skinned girl in a pink waterproof jacket has come from Preston; her luggage above us is addressed to Barcelona; she is on her way home after a year's absence. A young French airman who has fitted his back into the opposite corner seat is already trying to get off to sleep; he does not let his hands off the small canvas bag that is his only luggage.

Stephen and I manipulate the quarter mile of swaying corridor to the restaurant car. Here we order Indian tea; it comes in a little, porous, but insoluble bag attached to the lid of the metal pot. One can have tea anywhere and always it will give the same feeling of security, but in varying degrees—according to the background against which it is served. Now we are swinging through France, down the lighted tracks where all the night long men in berets and butcher-blue dungarees sweat rough wine and oil through their red and open pores; inside the train, young sleeker-skinned boys drink Coca-Cola and smear the pomade of violet grease further into their blue-black hair while they flick with supple wrists and boneless fingers through the pack of cards in front of them. We are like dry stalks of corn in front of all this— and the infusion we drink is as cerebral and exotic as the inhuman Chinese paintings of the Ming period. That is the outside of it, seen as it were from within. In fact, we are the clumsy and eccentric English who choose to drink a tisane fit only for invalids. We are here to be fleeced, only slightly less so since the arrival of the Americans.

Back in the carriage they are sleeping; we draw down the spring blinds to shade us from the glitter of station lights and signals that play on the shut-up faces of the other two. Turning and shifting from hip to hip, trying to sink a hollow in the resisting surface of the stuffed seat, now and then we slip away, weighted down by heavy lids. So the hours pass in spasmodic consciousness. When the blackness turns to slate gray, it is Toulouse.

A great shunting and banging of carriage doors. Gingerly we spread our few possessions along the seat in the hope of discouraging other passengers to the carriage, but it is only halfhearted and would not stand to any robust questioning. I think suddenly of something Cynthia said to me once when we went through the motions of the journey, in her dark back kitchen: "You always get a baby in at Toulouse."

It is impossible to slip away into half-sleep when the train is stationary and the corridors alive with

33

people who have been up since four o'clock with all their wits about them.

The airman wakes suddenly, looks out of the window, makes a dive for his grip, then hurls himself out onto the platform.

Stephen has not moved from his twisted position on the seat opposite; his eyes are half closed, but his breathing is slow and regular; his wiry black hair has risen to a point on the top of his head; he looks like a Tartar warrior—someone I have never seen before.

Suddenly there is a black solid mass in the doorway of the carriage, a thick woolen shawl unites a round head to shoulder and arm with no neck visible: "*Y a-t'il de la place messieurs—dames?*"

Stephen contracts from his starfish position, and I gather to my side the few small belongings to make a place. Four people file in; the last, a woman, carries an elderly whiskered dog.

Smoking this first cigarette of the day, bolt upright, head firm on my neck, fully awake, I take a close look at these Mediterranean roundheads. Two are Catalans, and the other two a couple from Perpignan. The French woman nurses in her tight-skirted lap the little terrier called Jooki. She is thickset and her skin has the texture of orange peel; her lips are pale but there is the heavy stain of frequent lipstick applied well above the natural outline of her mouth: there is a suggestion of small-time cabaret about her, of love and violence. One could hear the raucous voice lamenting after having brought down the jagged end of a bottle on the head of a lover: *"Je l'ai tué, tant pis pour moi."*

It is the almost unnoticeable development of the daylight on the strange carriageful and the moving scene beyond the window that give to the extraordinary sound coming from the mouth of the Frenchman a frightening almost inhuman quality. He is communicating; I can tell that from the soft words returned to him by his wife; but with each sound that he emits it is as if deep tubes filled up with air and the sound must choke its way up past dust and grit so that finally it is born, a tiny and unrecognizable squeak, quite separate and detached from the terrible effort it has cost to produce. He looks vaguely pirate with his flat cheekbones and narrow lidless eyes; around his neck there is a cotton scarf looped into a brass ring.

As the day matures, and the rain of northern and central France dries into dusty streaks on the windows, so we begin to know more of this couple. Their day-to-day reality becomes certified. The man with the colored scarf is a *mutilé de guerre*. His vocal cords were all blasted away by a shell—quite dumb he was for a long time in the base hospital, his wife tells us. Then they inserted into his neck a bright metal tube to replace the lost vocal cords; this hole, though healed, must remain open; the smuggler's scarf round his neck hides it from curious eyes (anyway he would be unable to support the pressure of a collar). All this she explains to me while he is standing outside in the corridor looking down at the incredible water along whose fringes the train makes its course, so unexpectedly blue to me and yet so much a part of his own tangerine-colored skin and his thick slower-moving blood.

When the train stops at Carcassone, he climbs down onto the line; and it is an act of neither boredom nor despair, but of love. Silently he watches the detached engines as they shunt backward and forward, the linesmen on their backs, legs curled in like helpless caterpillars as they tap at the stationary wheels with iron mallets. The drab peahen of a wife whose former brilliance she has wished to wash away, even to the silver-leaded line above her shaved eyebrows, sighs as she watches him; it has been a curious technique to acquire, this acceptance of life and death and mutilation, a kind of controlled artistry that goes beyond tears and prolonged feelings of regret. Now she sighs and says, *"Ah, c'était son métier avant la guerre, depuis tout ça il travail sur un journal."* Calmly she accepts that this sedentary occupation is the highest price that he could pay. When he returns to the carriage, they sit closer, there is a visible cleaving together of coarsely worked hands and yellowing skin; the dog-child Jooki springs to her lap to bind them closer, this time she does not bother to arrange the newspaper over her skirt for him to sit on.

It is getting hotter and whiter, and I have given up asking at every sight of the blue, *"Est-ce que c'est la Méditerranée?"*

We take off our coats and let the tiredness dissolve. The train has been cut down to a stubbly finger; it wriggles along the foothills of the Pyrenees, broad and pink-skinned at the base, rising to distant black peaks that disappear into the froth of clouds. I never expected these mountains to be so remote and yet so accessible. We are nearing the Spanish border and the French guard comes round to warn us that we will have to get out of the train at Port Bou.

So, it is Wednesday, and the first for Cynthia below the ground—the cold raw earth lined with evergreens. "Six feet of semi-detached will do me nicely, dear," I had heard her say often enough when she was looking for another smaller flat when their lease expired. At last this has been realized as a permanency.

Those who wait upon the act of death and its trappings, always say by way of consolation, like the anesthetist at an operation, "You will be the last to know about it." So one must expect that all the elaborate and well-mannered machinery will have gone into action before the awful fact dawns that one can no longer turn over and say something. By now, Cynthia must have accepted her fate; yet attached by the last tenuous earthly ties, perhaps her mind still floats into the warm far-reaching memories of Ibiza, the flowering pink oleanders and the heavy scent of oranges that I have never seen. How are all these things separated in her mind when there is no tomorrow and yesterday? What I do not know now, she will have had to forget by the time I have discovered it.

The girl from Barcelona is slipping back into her real identity, ceasing to be the shy foreigner "*au pair*"; she carries on a rapid conversation with the two Spaniards, breaking into throaty French when she wishes to make herself generally understood. After the train has pulled out of the mile-long tunnel that marks the border, she makes one last obeisance

in our direction, "We are in Spain," she says, showing a mouthful of even white teeth.

Quickly we go through the customs and passport
office, then round a rustic barrier that is no more than
a sheep pen to a platform where waits the train for
Barcelona; it is cinnamon brown, and that is the only
visible difference from the French train; but everywhere there is a heavy sweet smell, tuberoses or lilies,
yet there are no flower stalls to be seen. It must be
seeping out of the pores of the people themselves,
men and women alike—even from the numerous
members of the Civil Guard in their nettle-colored
uniforms and tricorn patent-leather hats.

I am trying to remember the exact flavor and tone
of Uncle Otway's drawing room in my grandmother's
London house, which he and Cynthia lived in before
his pension was cut. With this great sheet of plate
glass exposing us to the chromium-white heat, and
the prospect of three hours to Barcelona, it should be
easy to make the heavy Morris curtains draw tight
across the window and see again the red watered silk
on the walls, the curling baroque frames of the looking glasses flattening themselves like great golden
shells. . . . This was the height of a period of rich
fruition when my grandmother had just died, leaving little else but a legacy of beautiful objects, the

brief moment before the rot insinuates itself beneath the pink bloom and attracts the pretty blue flies at first one by one, until they are a black cloud settling on the first fur of decay as it worms its way to the surface.

After Cynthia had been married to my uncle for five years, she began in my eyes to assume a proportion; that is to say, in relation to the other members of my family. From being a pretty little woman, the kind of mother I would have chosen for myself at the age of fourteen, who later became the recipient of my many hopes and confidences, she had changed to My Aunt, the person most closely connected with the man who had sentenced me to the St. Thomas Secretarial College, and, when that failed, to a high stool and a metronome that beat against the faulty rhythm of unwilling children whose parents aspired no higher than that they should be able to strum for pleasure at a party. At this time, Cynthia walked about the area of the cold and unmanageable flat to which they had lately moved, in a loose silk gown edged with dead wisps of marabou; the skirt strained and billowed outward over her big belly on which she wore a bow, partly as decoration but rather more as a signpost to indicate what was already obvious.

In this way it was impossible to ignore the increase of her size. They used to refer to it, my uncle and she, as "the sprog"; and he would pat the bow as the ears of a good retriever, rejoicing at the distention and the great amount of water in which his offspring floated.

For myself, it was difficult to know exactly where to join in. I knew nothing about babies except what I had read in the *St. John's Ambulance Manual*, which hardly dealt with pregnancy at all but more with the emergencies of sudden birth. I used to try and pitch my voice to an everyday tone, as if the pat knowledge I could produce for their benefit was a proof of my unsqueamish acceptance of the mystery; but all the time I felt that their eyes watched me and pitied me for my incoherence and lovelessness.

I was over twenty-five, and I had come within the core of myself to know that I could never successfully make a real contact with another human being. I knew, without the exercise of much imagination, what happened to women like myself—nothing, except perhaps the increasing weakness of my bad eye, which lately seemed to have lost some of its elasticity and power to focus, mainly through neglect to persevere with the exercises, so that it now looked often into the blank wall of my nose almost with relief. Soon the skin of my face would weather and redden, as it already showed signs of doing: the pinkness of health, my mother had called it—while I could only think of the small windfalls in the grass that shrivel into rosy immortality because they have never tasted the real sap of life, which would have made them rich and rotting at the dip of a branch.

I had just sufficient self-knowledge to assess the extent of my own talent; but I could not accept it as it was. What at sixteen had promised to be the one thing that would protect me and put me far beyond the reaches of human despair had gradually shown itself to be uncoordinated and intermittent, like a small jewel that has always been hopelessly flawed and can have no intrinsic value except in the eyes of those who seek effect and not perfection. I knew now without a doubt that I would never perform as a serious pianist; that the best engagement I could hope for would be second-rate. All this was evident to me, and yet it was my uncle Otway whom I outwardly blamed for destroying my self-confidence and making me a flop.

To earn my living I taught piano in a convent school.

One day after tea at home, I said to my mother: "What do you suppose it would cost to get my eye done?"

As I spoke, I was thinking of the courage it would cost me, and the pain (they do not give more than a local anesthetic for this operation, since complete consciousness is essential). I did not expect her to answer my question at once but to chatter a little, perhaps go into the problem of when would be the most convenient time to have it done. When she spoke, it seemed preposterous, as if it were some other being that spoke and not my mother. "I don't see what you've got to worry about," she had said. "You've got on very well as you are; your old eye hasn't stopped you getting good jobs. If it had been a public life, well, that would have been different. As it is, with a good brim to your hat, I defy anyone to notice anything wrong with you."

When she had finished I was sinking into the depths of my despair. Incoherent and seething with malformed resentments, I shouted: "That's what *I* said, when I was sixteen and afraid. You're using my own words to torture me."

Then she had changed again and assumed another character: "Poor little Hatty," she cried, "I wish I'd had the money; if only I'd had the money." Her weeping was so overwhelming that I was diverted for a little while and set about consoling her for her loss.

I carried this conversation to Cynthia and laid it

at her feet; for the moment I forgot the embarrassment of her fat tummy. "What can she have meant?" As I recalled the scene the motions of horror and indignation mounted; I sat rocking myself backward and forward on a kitchen chair: "Can she want me to remain like this, grow old and become a freak?"

Cynthia could not really help me, or so it seemed at the time. She did not attempt to analyze or probe, but smoothed it over, spiriting me away through the loopholes she had made for herself into the past, out of the ugly room in which we sat. "When I was in Ibiza, dear, it must have been—let me see, the summer of 1928—I never had to lift a finger to do anything for myself; the sweetest little señora used to wash all my undies and keep me as fresh as a daisy, and *all* for love."

Her dry little laugh, as she stood at the deep old-fashioned sink washing the cups, showed up the misty glass of the windows. "Just a bit of sun," she sighed, "is all it takes to show up the drabness and holes in the covers."

I felt pity take shallow root in me, which was what I suppose she intended by way of a deflection. I noticed suddenly the mushroom-colored patches beneath her eyes and that every time she bent down or reached upward a little knot of blue veins stood out on her forehead. Below in the street the plane trees were in full leaf. To those who looked up into the green-veined canopy, there was no indication of the thick coating of dust that we could see from the window.

Now, with the easing of my hurt, I thought about the light drifts of underclothes strewn over the floor, of Cynthia slipping her white feet over the mosaic of tiles; the smiling little servant who, like an ancient wool gatherer, would move from pile to pile restoring order.

And now with the depletion of my uncle's income, a retired lieutenant-colonel's disability pension, all these past scenes were hardening into the immobile permanency of picture postcards—stills, like lantern slides, that required only a trick of light to bring them to life. There was little sign of ease or leisure in Cynthia's life at that time; only occasionally could it be detected in the supple flexing of the wrist as she held, poised for an instant, my grandmother's boat-shaped silver teapot over an empty cup.

The heat increases. We are inside a furnace with the damper out. I am immensely thirsty and Stephen smilingly offers me the last drop of the wine that we have carried so far; it has undergone another change and now tastes acid and astringent, like a vile tonic. It makes me want to spit, but I find that I have practically no saliva.

Thinking about the approaching city—white, as I imagine it will be, but not in any way smooth and lit from within, but rather more opaque and chalky, with dust rising in the streets in thick hot clouds at the stirring of a wheel—all this produces in me a certain inertia and predisposition to be led:

> *Stretch out your hand in the dark*
> *It will be taken.*

At twenty-five then, that must have been the moment, the peak of the affinity when it seemed that Cynthia had it in her hands to bring out the sun from behind a cloud and focus it on me at will.

It was late summer, on the fringes of autumn, with the leaves still fast upon the trees; yet here and there a cobweb skeleton leaf in the grass showed where the prematurely aged had escaped even the process of decay; there was no sign as yet of the damp brown drifts, only the perfection of this in-between season.

Cynthia was within two weeks of expecting her child. I had bought myself a floppy leghorn hat to wear at the party.

"We must have one last fling before I go in," she had said, and we had worked through the list of names as she calculated the quantities of food and drink that she would have to order.

"Teddy is always such a help with the difficult ones," she had said, not so much as a reiteration of ancient maternal pride but as a statement of almost filial dependency, which must have been fostered by the very instability and precariousness of her financial position with my uncle.

"I wish you two could make a hit together. At least you could go to concerts; it isn't as if he had anyone else in tow." Her efforts to produce family unity had been boundless. Ted and I had met frequently in a neutral background: a flat that was as much his mother's as my uncle's. It did not bring us any closer.

He had never heard me play the piano, and I had nothing with which to disprove my inadequacy. "Hatty has the L.R.A.M.," he used to inform people. "She's *so* musical." But this announcement was nearly always in relation to having just been to "an out-of-this-world and magical performance" by someone like Cortot or Pachmann.

Slowly, however, I began to accustom myself to the fruity tenor of his voice; the damped-down yellow duck's-tails that seemed always the same length; the area of his emotional experience that spanned the great unknown jungles from Torrington Square, where he lived, to the World's End, Chelsea.

We had, at the suggestion of his mother, made one or two Sunday excursions into the green belts of outer London.

A terrible day, I remember, at Boreham Wood, overshadowed all the way by the living presence of George Orwell. We had arrived at the village after a long and silent walk through the Hertfordshire lanes. Ted had hardly opened his mouth, and this unnatural behavior on his part set me to cast about wildly like a madwoman for something to say. I already anticipated the kindly inquiry from Cynthia when we got back: "Well, what did you see, what did you talk about?" I *had* to find the one thing that would show deep thought and observation, an apologia for the humiliating void in my mind. In the difficult gymnastic of getting across a high stile—it did not enter his head to help me—I stopped, and called out to where he stood in the middle of the field, "The swallow's are flying low, that means rain, doesn't it?"

He did not answer my question; he did not even turn and laugh at the peculiar ineptness of the remark. He merely walked on toward the main road, and I thought: perhaps he is afraid for me because of my nervousness and twenty-five shriveled years. Or perhaps he never heard.

We had arrived at Boreham Wood at the moment when the street lamps were turning everything a harsh yellow, their broad shafts cutting into the sooty evening.

In the teashop there were two other couples besides ourselves, and it was here that Ted began suddenly to orate and soliloquize. "You can see that shrimp of a girl over there in the fawn belted coat, Hatty?" and when I turned in the wrong direction "No, not that one; over there with the brown-haired chap. Well, I will tell you what he is thinking as he watches her rubbing together her chapped hands, self-consciously spinning into view the tiny sparklet on her left hand that she has lately acquired—a ray of hope. . . . He is peeling away the years ahead until he sees her an upholstered, better-molded Hilda (that's more than probably her name), not the uneven bit of girl who always suffers from extremes of heat or cold, but a subdued impervious woman with neatly coiled hair, in a well-fitted jumper suit sitting behind the electroplated teapot and doing the honors without a grizzle or a smile. . . . My God; it makes me sick, all this cannibalistic gentility! Bourgeois clutter—and what is it all for, I ask you?"

After this spate he collapsed, fell inward into his own thoughts, devoured two doughnuts, and left me mercifully on my own, isolated and unnoticed.

So there was Ted then, at the top of the list among the family beside my own name; at least we had the barren fields of our incompatibility between us, which made us better than strangers.

I arrived late at the party—the prerogative of the very worldly, or the uncertain—and steered my way on new high heels toward Cynthia, who sat in a Victorian nursing chair. She bloomed out of it like a blue hydrangea. There was a tall man standing beside her, and he had to bend himself almost double in order to reach her ear.

After I had kissed her she took my hand and, giving a slight tug to this strange man's coat to draw his attention, said, "This is an old friend of the family, Hatty. Jasper Lomax; my niece Hatty Skelton, Isobel's child."

He straightened himself and smiled vaguely at me; then I noticed that he was quite old. Apart from the thick hair that might have been prematurely gray, there were deep trenches in the flesh that ran from nose to mouth; his cheeks had fallen away like canvas tents that had lost their supports. "Jasper has known us all for a very long time. You knew Jim, too, didn't you?"

At the mention of my dead father's name I looked at this strange man more closely and with greater interest. She did not give him time to reply then, but with "I'll leave you two together; there must be so much for you to talk about," she sailed across the room like a small galleon floating through her guests.

"Let me see," Jasper Lomax was saying, "I knew your father in India, yes, but I think we've met before too, if I remember rightly."

He had a thin squeaky laugh that seemed to have no connection with the broad high shoulders and big sunburned face: "I called on your mother once, it must have been on a leave during the fourteen–eighteen war; she was living in a pretty little house near Victoria Square. *We* were introduced and I was allowed to crawl with you in your pen; you were a tough little blighter and tried to kick me out with the points of your leather boots."

"Shoes," I said, instinctively correcting, then regretted it.

Yet he seemed not to mind and went on talking in the same tone. "Oh, well, in my youth it was boots for boys and girls alike, so I expect it always will be,

51

in my mind." He had not spoken in the least sharply nor seemed put out by my too quick interruption, and I was grateful for the steady continuance of his reminiscence. In a way it forged the first frail link, kindled a hidden warmth with someone I had never seen before, but who was remotely connected with my family and childhood. That was the beginning.

I remember so clearly the beautiful translucence of his saxe-blue eyes, the healthy brown pouches that ripened into the fine veined cheeks. I looked out, it seemed for the first time, with the control and focus of both my eyes.

"Look here," Jasper said to me after we had been separated and met again later in the evening, during which time I had never let the sight of his big gray head escape me, "won't you take pity on an old duffer and have a bite of dinner with me one night?"

I could afford at that moment, and I suppose that therein lay my strength, to register surprise, minute disgust at the ugly picture that those words created in my mind. "I'm in the middle of my Royal Academy exams," I said. "I teach music at a school, I expect Cynthia's told you." (I imagined in both arrogance and humility that he would know all about me from my uncle and his wife.) "But I'd like to, though, when the rush is over." I watched the flicker of interest in his eyes; I had guilelessly held back in this game of manners, not jumped like a pup at the sight of a sugar lump.

He said, "Well, that will be simply splendid. I shall look forward to it. Will you take it that I shall be in touch with you through your aunt and uncle?" He gave a strangely old-fashioned bow that was as becoming to his height and age as it was self-conscious in its precision.

It was not what I had expected—this cheerful acquiescence; nevertheless I went away from the meeting relieved and a little satisfied with myself. Really it was cheek of the old boy—he must be at least fifty if he was both Father's and Uncle Ot's contemporary; yet this very fact, I supposed, was reason enough for him to ask me out.

A few days later I discovered that he was a distinguished traveler. I saw his name in the paper as guest of honor at a dinner given by the Royal Society of Archaeology. Seeing the words "Jasper Lomax," separated from the reality of his body, was the magical turning point; age fell away from him, leaving only the bare bones of manliness, the high-arched eagle nose and the imprisoned bravery within the skull.

It was nearly two weeks after the party that I had the sudden and impulsive desire to telephone him at his club. He was not there, they told me; he called in only occasionally for letters and messages. I put down the receiver quickly before they had time to ask me my name. Like many people who are unaccustomed to constant use of the telephone, I endowed it with an extra sense: I was certain that the black mouth could *see*. Sick with shame at the boldness of my action, I imagined that the call could be traced; I could have bitten my tongue out and beaten myself. Now, at each subsequent ring, I waited for the frightful snub that would be delivered to me through my unknowing mother, for I was determined to never to touch the instrument again.

Jasper telephoned the following Sunday just before luncheon. "I've been thinking," he said, "that your prison sentence must be nearly up; what about next Wednesday? I've been lent a car for the rest of the month. We could go for a spin down to Maidenhead, have dinner at Skindles, and look at the river. September's a fine month for the river. What do you say?" He did not mention anything about my abortive call to his club. Perhaps he had not been told.

Never to have the exact knowledge of one's position is the predicament of human frailty. Compassless, to see the beckoning lights, one advances to find that there is nothing there but a reflection in the deep-rooted blackness. I remember the third of my closely spaced meetings with Jasper.

We were traveling down the spine of Campden Hill. Just at the bottom, taking the right bend from Phillimore Gardens into Argyll Road, the taxi lurched, bringing into sudden close contact the fine granulated texture of tweed with my bare arm; his front teeth grazed the middle of my upper lip, my neck arched stiffly backward against the granite plumpness of the black upholstery. I felt like a rabbit, hypnotized in the full glare of the headlamps. Instinctively I drew up my knees, rigid as the ancient burial position of the Incas; I could not move even after the taxi had straightened on its course and Jasper, insidious as an outgoing tide, had withdrawn into his own corner.

Out on the pavement it was bright and blue, the same as yesterday and the day before. Jasper pushed his large-brimmed hat to the back of his head with a reckless gaiety and said, "Well, my sweet, when shall I see you?" As he spoke, I could hear my mother's voice pounding in the back of my mind: Men, men, men. Men in their cups. *In vino caritas*. Don't you believe it. Don't make yourself cheap. Don't go to a man's rooms alone. Don't give your photograph. They will only make a caricature of it, draw in a moustache, hold it up to ridicule in their messes or wardrooms.

"Why are you looking so perplexed?" Jasper's voice came to me now through the spider webs of fears and doubts; he took my hand, "I can't stop now, but ring me early tomorrow. Promise?"

He was drawing away, eyes already calculating the distance from one side of the road to the other, waiting for the two cars and a bicycle to pass on before crossing.

"Jasper," I called out suddenly, "tell me why you want to see me again?"

He had nearly reached the other side of the road. When he had mounted the other pavement, he turned to face me. The road was now quite empty of people and traffic, yet he cupped his hands to his mouth to amplify his voice: "Let's say, because *I love you*."

The words carried right into the soft part of my brain and stuck there like three neutral stones. I suppose that I must have stood there with my mouth open, my bad eye focusing all over the place in an effort to materialize him again in the gap which he had left. This was the first time that anyone had ever said these words to me; the first time, and they were no more active than fizzy lemonade. I wanted to reach out and extricate them from the smutty stucco frontages of the ugly houses, save them from the smell of petrol and the dust-thick sun of two o'clock of that September afternoon.

Two-fifteen P.M. and Barcelona. The journey has been a slow and glaring exposure; our carriage filling up at every step with brown glistening people; curious smiling faces, the widespread skirts settling like sheathed umbrellas; then the fluttering of their pleated paper fans to stir up the atmosphere and give a feeling of movement.

In my lilac angora jumper, my face suffused to a sugar pink, I am like a decorated fondant that will quite soon begin to melt into the deeper, more treacly textures of the skins around me.

The Catalan girl has at last relinquished her rain-proof jacket; the tops of her arms, in spite of Preston, are still tobacco brown in color; she speaks not a word of English now. Only once she leans forward to offer me a Capstan from the supply she has bought on the channel steamer.

If I have ever supposed that Barcelona would hold within its city walls anything approaching the elements of coziness, either cobbled street or with-drawn courtyard, where one could sit in comfortable security and absorb to one's capacity, I am grievously mistaken.

We are hurled out of the high-stepped train onto the platform, alive as a beach shelved with a fish catch. I realize that after we have said goodbye to the girl from Preston there will not even be the possibility of making vocal contact with anyone. Stephen is ahead of me. "Where can you suggest we get dinner?" he asks, as we use the rounded edges of our baggage to push our way to the barrier.

She smiles back at him blankly—a little doll with the taut strings of her box barely snipped: "I'm afraid we don't eat out in restaurants in our family, but I will ask someone in a minute."

I turn away under this echoing arched dome of glass, this white-hot glittering palace, and mentally detach myself from Stephen and the girl, who are carrying on a rapid conversation in French. The idea of the empty hours of the siesta that will be at our disposal, the liberty to go to any far hidden corner of this great commercial city, is like commitment to a rudderless boat without anchor.

There is a commotion of voices quite near me; a quick fire of question and answer. Stephen and the girl have been joined by a ferret-faced boy across whose peaked cap is written "Pension Termino." He is smiling and shrugging his shoulders, indifferent, yet insistent: the perfect patience of an angler, as we are later to discover. He speaks a harsh, inaccurate French and some broken English, but it is an element of contact between us. I do not like the scaly quality of his reddish eyes; they remind me of a lizard's whose low temperature can never be increased even on the most sun-baked wall. The girl is shaking our hands and saying finally, "He will take you to a place where you can get dinner for twenty-five pesetas each."

I want suddenly to hold on to her and say, "Thank you, but no, no, no." But I am too late, and she is swallowed up in the crowd.

The boy now has our bags and is leading us out of the station. I start to speak to him in French, cutting through the dust and phlegm that has collected at the back of my throat, forcing up the words, to discover where he is taking us. It is quite simple, he says; he understands perfectly what I say, and is taking us straight to the hotel of his *patron*.

"Stephen, the shipping office, you won't let him forget the shipping office?" I insist, some of the urgency already draining out of me; he answers that everything will be all right and that there is plenty of time. He, too, appears hypnotized by the penetrating glare; so we move inevitably down the half-empty, streetcar-lined streets. We follow this strange youth almost in a trance, yet all the time I know in the back of my mind that there is something I will have to insist on—later.

How to get over the hump of the afternoon? It is too hot to walk and I wish now that I had not worn high-heeled shoes. The thing to do after this little journey will be to find somewhere cool where we can sit and drink.

We penetrate a dark entrance through an archway on the far side of a big, tired square. There is an inner courtyard and, hanging from the walls like giant creepers, a complex of iron stairways. On the third floor up, we find a glass door with the words "Pension Termino" painted across it.

Inside the little lobby of the *pension*, we cause a great deal of excitement; the boy, who is the trusted fisherman on the platform for the incoming train from France, hands us over. I notice that the bright black eyes of the *patron* and a full-breasted serving girl flit from our canvas luggage to our new portable typewriter. They indicate an empty table; and the girl starts rapidly to alter the position of the cloth, so that the stains will be less noticeable, and to lay out the knives and forks.

Stephen insists in French that we have already

eaten on the train; that we will drink some cold lemonade. There are Victorian glass cruets on the table filled to the brim with oil and red wine vinegar. Everyone around us is eating fried eggs; they scoop out the yolk and fill it with pools of olive oil: it is not to be wondered that their skins should be so glistening, their hair as flat and shining as the silk top hats of city businessmen.

The lemonade is colorless and cold, thick spoonfuls of sugar like fingers of frost stick to the inside of the tall glass; it is the most cooling drink that I have ever had. We leave the little hotel with the understanding that we will return for dinner at six: the boy, who is called Ramón, has taken off his uniform hat; we are no longer of interest to him as he looks concentratedly toward the kitchen, awaiting his three o'clock meal that is part of the payment for his labors at the station.

We shall sit in the open until four o'clock when the shipping office opens. There is a café on the pavement—a few iron chairs scattered round a bar counter. Under the shadowy arches of the square, there are all levels of beauty and nightmare. We sit drinking more of the colorless sweet lemonade and watching.

Down one sharpened vista, we can see the staffs

from the big commercial houses round the docks taking their lunch in shadowed respectability. In the near vicinity, almost at our feet, there is the scattered and squalid refuse from a one-windowed shop that sells only fish. Outside here, the people are like to the mutilated debris hidden away in the arches; fishes' heads, with their mouths still open in a last effort at survival, and the wooden-legged no-eared riffraff who work as they can on the cargo boats. There are people always in life who accept the very act of drawing breath as a gift of God, and each sense or limb that is denied them only serves to accentuate this gift. Finally, they become as disembodied angels, geniuses or idiots—almost incapable of communicating to the outside world. We should give to their material support, but they owe us something, too; we must reach out to the ends of their poor bound stumps and feel with our bare fingers the true gift of profit and loss.

The boy Ramón comes out into the street and recognizes us. Without invitation he sits down at our table and orders for himself black coffee and cognac; there is something permanent in this attachment, and Stephen says that we must soon go and book our places on the boat for Ibiza. "*A bientôt*," we call out; but to Ramón this is no farewell.

Now we walk without knowledge of our direction, slightly behind Ramón until he turns round and points up to a tall spire; through the narrow gothic streets we follow him to a sandy space when suddenly we are at the bottom of the shallow flight of steps leading to the great entrance of the cathedral. Wedged in between other buildings, the mass of creepers gives to the ancient stonework a feeling of preserved ruin.

Inside, it is like sudden blindness after the glare; not a beam of light until the eye accustoms itself and discovers the rows of spluttering candles in front of the shrines and the red swinging lamp at a side altar.

I do not yet understand the arrested Latin philosophy that is Spain. I do not understand the essence of their being: the blood-letting and the blood-staying that is part of the bread of their existence. It is perhaps a deeper faith and acceptance, that goes beyond the elaborate traceries of our northern minds. All the time in Spain it is the pitting of strength against strength; and this technique is developed to such a point of perfection that the loser must not witness his defeat. Bulls, royal-blooded, stampeding and prancing, wait ultimately only for the jeweled dagger between the eyes. Blue-quilled cocks with sharpened beaks and pared claws spread their wholeness over the small sandy pitch, and nearly always expire side by side, their victory assessed only by points—after they are dead.

As we come out into the light again, the boy Ramón drops a centavo into the upturned palm of a beggar: "*Mieux que je donne aux pauvres,*" he mutters, "*que j'aille a la messe chaque jour.*" With this parable on charity, niggling doubts of his innocence begin to disperse.

"Gaudí," I say, suddenly spirited. "How far to the Sagrada Família?" For this strangely hideous temple sprouting stone cacti on its spires, of which I have seen so many pictures, cannot be far to reach. Ramón does not answer my question; his eyes empty of interest. "Gaudí," he says, "very old man."

Stephen is on another track; with smiles and hand movements he is asking: "And do they have dancing before the high altar on feast days, *pour les fêtes de l'église?*"

Pinpoints of interest return to the boy's eyes; the words have struck some chord, let loose a deep longing in the thin hard mind of Ramón. "*Fêtes,*" he says like a word of exultation. "*Feria.*"

Suddenly we are in a taxi, sailing away from the crazy toppling streets into wider spaces; tree-lined roads rise out of the rest of ancient stone, a feeling of being above sea level replaces the city claustrophobia. The taxi slows down at a turnstile and there is a roar of loudspeakers as the shock of amplified music booms in our ears. We are at the entrance of a huge industrial fair.

"*La feria!*" shouts the boy, joggling his head to the music; and Stephen digs into his pocket to find the nine pesetas for our three entrance tickets.

Inside, it is how I have always imagined Olympia; a place I have avoided going to all my life in London, but am incapable of missing the first day in Barcelona.

A whole hour of deafening stupefaction; now and then a glass of warm beer at Ramón's request; then we are in a gray upholstered taxi, swinging back to the Pension Termino for our early dinner.

One last drink in the square before we go up to eat: the opaque clouds of absinthe are stained coral red by the addition of grenadine, before the water.

At the quayside there are two white boats rocking like birds on the sheet of water. Ramón pushes us toward the nearest, and we walk quickly, for it is nearly seven, the time scheduled for it to sail. He goes before us to speak to a woman clerk who sits in a closed-in kiosk; then, turning round, he beams a reprieve: "*Le bateau ne part qu'à onze heures,*" he sings, swinging his narrow hips and clipping two coins together for the sound of castanets; *"ce soir vous verrez le joli cabaret, vous aimez le flamenco, Madame?"*

Suddenly I know that this is the moment of insistence that I have been waiting for all day; simultaneously I see the word "Palma" painted in black on this waiting boat. Running forward, I shout to the woman, *"Ibiza, le bateau pour Ibiza!"*

She becomes galvanized into action and jumps to her feet; then she points excitedly to the other boat whose funnels are belching clouds of smoke.

We run like the wind and the boy with us. The decks of the boat are black with passengers and the gangway is beginning to soar upward. The crew throw across a plank when they see our hurried approach; we hurl our luggage, all but the typewriter, onto the center decks; then, with care and amidst loud cheers from the other passengers, we walk the plank.

The vanquished Ramón shrugs his shoulders and withdraws; he has after all only lost what he so nearly won, on points, seconds on the clock. Stephen leans forward over the rails and holds out a crumpled fifty-peseta note. He takes it quickly without a word, then disappears into the crowd, not to tempt providence further.

How can one ever know the extent of one's own or another's victory in the hidden battles of the heart? Words and gestures extracted from their context become inflated to gigantic significance, then later as precise and moribund as a flower specimen pressed into the leaves of a book when the life-giving stamens are blurred to a small yellow stain over the print.

I had thought at the beginning of my love for Jasper that it would sustain a quality of agelessness and endurance; that it would become finally as sweetly preserved as a bowl of dried petals, from which I would be able to draw strength until I died.

Cynthia, who was more knowledgeable of the past, knew differently. She was also forward-looking.

I played a game like this: "Of course, there's nothing in it as far as I'm concerned," when she chided me about my beau. "I only hope he doesn't take it too seriously, it's so nice to have him for a friend."

Whether she accepted these insincerities or not, I never knew; plump as a pouter pigeon, in spite of the removal of a ten-pound son to the cradle in the corner of the room, she was well enough padded against emotional draft to be able to reply, "Well, I think he's very taken with you dear, but you know what *men* are."

I, in fact, knew nothing; not even remotely to what she alluded. I thought in my wisdom and hopeful innocence that there must be some hidden answer to what people were really like contained in a simple word. It was like searching for a magical incantation, for the essence and elixir of life, believing that it still existed. At ten years old, my uncle Ot had answered me when I begged a cigarette for myself, "Go into the garden and find for me a flower that has all the colors of the rainbow in its petals and that smells of Christmas turkey at its heart, and I will give you a cigarette in exchange."

Now, Uncle Otway reflected what should have been my mother's prerogative, had she been more fully aware of my new relationship. Having in a sense produced the rabbit out of the hat, he now sought to force it back. He was thunderously disapproving of my meetings with Jasper, whom he would no longer invite to his flat. When he saw me alone it seemed that metaphorically he was trying to force me back into a cradle that I had never been particularly anxious to leave.

"You're a bloody little fool to play around with

old Jasper. I happen to know more about him than you do. You seem to forget that both your father and I were with him in Quetta before you were born."

I was outraged by the violence of his attack, thrown suddenly into a seething whirlpool of doubts and resentments.

Ted was about to witness these scenes, sometimes hovering in the background with Cynthia while the arguments took place. Now and then he would mildly tease me about Jasper, but I think his feelings were well disposed and for my own part I felt easier and more communicative in his presence than I had ever done before.

One day before tea, my uncle produced from a shelf a book containing something, he said, that would interest me very much. Uncertain of his humor, for there had always been a horrific element in his jokes, I waited tensely.

"It's a poem," he said at last, as if by prolonging the uncertainty he would have us more fully at his mercy when the time came—"it's a poem and the poet, if you have retained your education, should not be unknown to you; as to the subject, let it apply to whom it may." Then he cleared his throat and boomed:

"Men, some to business, some to pleasure take,
  But every woman is at heart a rake."

There was no doubt in my mind at the time but that the attack was against me. Cynthia and Ted snickered into their teacups, while Uncle Ot, having made his point, rubbed his hands jovially together and cut deeply into the slab of fruit cake.

I was, I remember, paralyzed with misery and self-consciousness, desperately intent on controlling, without the use of a handkerchief, the tears that were already beginning to slip down my nose. I stared into the hard brilliance of the central light bulb until it cured and dazzled me. But that was the end of it, I thought, as far as I was concerned: I would never be able to ask Cynthia for her advice again, now she had definitely established herself as my uncle's pawn.

The last thing she had said to me as I got my coat on was: "Well, you really do ask for it, Hatty, with that soulful look and mop of Rossettian hair. Your uncle doesn't mean any harm; he takes the stuffing out of all of us. Have a heart now."

Ted came out into the street with me and we walked some of the way home. "What a terrible pair," I said, "quite heartless, like a couple of stone images." I forgot about Cynthia being his mother, and went on fanatically: "Do you think it's insane jealousy that makes Uncle Ot go on as he does? A kind of incestuous affection; he tries to kiss me at the front door in a—I don't know how to describe it—lingering way. Last week he hung over the lid of the piano when I was playing a Liszt variation."

Ted stood back on his worn-down heels and laughed at me with real pleasure and surprise. "You're coming out, Hatty, really you are. I always imagined that nothing much went on in your noodle except a ditty-bag of old-maidish fancies and a sentimental attachment to the better-known arias."

Strangely, I did not mind it when he said this; I was buoyed up, insulated against everything by my present obsession. "What do fathers and uncles want of their offspring, Ted? Does Uncle expect me to go on like a perpetual schoolgirl, bringing my lessons home after tea for all eternity?"

But he did not answer my question, nor did he try. "It's perfect Cocteau," was all he said as he climbed onto his bus and was carried away toward the Euston Road.

Cynthia tried several times in the near future to smooth over the upheaval. She did not refer directly to the scene, but tried in her usual way to divert my feelings of resentment toward her and Uncle, by returning to a neutral territory that was as much a pleasure for her to recall as it was for me to hear about. I think that she regarded this island of Ibiza as a kind of emotional sanctuary. "You mustn't worry too much about the present, Hatty; the only consolation I can give you from my great age is that everything diminishes with time, unless you want to keep it alive. When I had my job teaching in Barcelona at the language school, I was a bit like you. I had a marvelous time. Mind you, I had to scrape a bit to send back the money to Mother, who was looking after Ted." She drifted away, forgetting, it seemed, the purpose of her reminiscence. "I was in my early thirties and I never expected anything to happen that would change my way of life. I thought I would go on teaching English in Spain and coming home once a year until I'd saved up enough to settle down in a place of my own; in Ibiza, I hoped."

I remember her now as she had been when I first saw her. The picture that had been taken with the unclouded lenses of a fourteen-year-old's eyes had gained in the intervening years another dimension; I could see now the might-have-been; the little touches of English chintz and pottery that she must have added to her hotel bedroom to make it like home; the warm nest of spinsterly living into which she would eventually wind herself. So often this is the way with solitary Englishwomen of character who retire abroad: they harden like the autumnal beads at their throat into hard little wax pellets that no heat will ever melt again; they turn into a self-supporting wholesome substance that can never take anything in, nor be taken in, again.

At this moment then, when there was still a foot space in the door, my uncle Otway must have stepped into Cynthia's life.

"When I first saw him, dear," she told me, "I thought he was the most wonderful creature I had ever set eyes on; from that moment I knew that nothing could ever be the same for me again." She bloomed backward now, and it was as if this second flowering that had come to her so long ago in Ibiza had now reached its second summer with the first shrivelings of autumn touching it.

It was late afternoon, and the delicate, work-reddened hands poised like scarlet butterflies over the tea table. The moss roses painted on the Swansea wall plates came suddenly alive in her usually pale cheeks; the morning star that she grew in pots on the windowsill was reflected for an instant in her stone-colored eyes. "I loved him without reservation; I was quite certain of myself from the first moment I set eyes on him. Oh, there had been others! In fact, there was someone else, about at that time, of whom I was quite fond, but that's another story. Otway didn't ask me to marry him for several years, but it didn't seem to matter; I was content just to be near him and to catch the crumbs."

I thought, looking at her then, after she had finished speaking, that it had not been art or craft that she had used in her gradual envelopment of my uncle, but indestructible patience that went beyond the boundaries of pride and hope.

Jasper, when he had begun to notice the absence of invitations to my uncle's flat, began to develop with me a technique of communication that was founded on disapproval. The material for this interplay was the intricacies and variabilities of the relationship between Uncle Otway and Cynthia. He would strike up an attitude of shocked amazement when I reported that the flat was full of young women in whom I was sure my uncle took more than just a casual interest. Egged on by his applause, I began out of the substance of my resentment to fabricate scenes of my middle-aged uncle surrounded by these prancing fillies; and each time Jasper would roar with laughter, giving a feeling of completion that somehow, at other times, our relationship seemed to lack.

"The fellow's a joke," he would say, dispelling the age gap between us, strengthening any doubts as to the seriousness of his intentions toward me. "But by Jove, he ought to be horsewhipped for fooling around, treating Cynthia like that."

I was on these occasions exultant, drunk with hope, for there is no feeling headier than the whole-hearted disapproval of one's neighbor. In this case too, a further miracle was effected: the impossible bridging of the years that separate one generation of a family from another. Normally it is not possible to treat someone of one's parents' age as an equal; but with Jasper it was different. With our jokes and underhand criticism of his contemporary, my uncle, we became like little children huddled together at the top of the nursery stairs, eavesdropping and snickering at the grown-ups.

That was our first summer together, the first taste for me of primrose warmth deepening to the heavy sweetness of honey. The flowering trees at Kew and Hampton Court were like top-heavy and wilting brides whose lacy whiteness clung, then slipped from their green shoulders and scattered over the fine yellow gravel of the paths, so neatly reminiscent of graveyard and hospital walk.

Jasper had, too, what I found to be an added

fascination—a sharp eye for the quaintly detailed, even though it be slightly macabre. He went to enormous pains to point out to me, in the London Museum, the rusty smudges that still showed on the blue woven singlet worn by Charles I at his execution: "That's the place where the blood actually spurted when the axe fell." He had passed his thin pointed tongue along his lips, and we had moved to the next display case. Then, picking out the little humped boots, "They say the fellow only had feet the size of an infant's," he had explained. "They had to weigh him down with lead like a spinning top to keep him upright."

The weight of the slowly moving ship easing its way out of the harbor of Barcelona stirs beneath us. Stephen is quick to mark out a place for us with the luggage on the raised surface of the battened-down hatch; here at least we will be able to stretch out without being walked over. A group of blond men and women establish themselves in the far corner; with blankets and a small spirit stove, they show up the flaws in our improvised travel equipment. We discover that they are German.

The vanishing city grows golden in the sunset, all the white roofs and walls touched with fire, unbelievably mellow and tender in outline; the remembrance of the glare and gritty discomfort of the streets is washed away.

The wind is like a cloth of silk; it has no sharp edges. We give ourselves up to the broad iron band across the hatch and allow it to divide one end of our spines from the other. Later, with the excitement ebbing and the drop in temperature of the blood, I find that it is almost impossible to get off to sleep; I roll my feet in a woolen cardigan and cover my shoulders with an overcoat, but the cold has settled into me and the garments slip away time after time from my rigid, unfeeling limbs. Stephen is breathing steadily at my side, his loosely tucked overcoat emanates constant warmth; he does not even stir from the contact of my cold hand.

Occasionally sheeted over by a thin layer of sleep, I imagine that I can still look up into the white bubbly surface of the top deck that makes a roof over us; then straight out through the railings over the black sea. Waking sharply only when the coat slips off, I realize it to have been the light of a dream, for the ship is wrapped in darkness but for one weak bulb left burning in the saloon. With this imposed solitude—the last person left awake—it is but a step to being the last person left alive in the world. How easy to slip silently through the wide railings unheeded; in the morning, unaccounted for. Like Cynthia after her first night in the earth, the waking could be as unexpected.

In the weak light of the dawn there appears against the sky the shadow of a long mountain range; gray and precise as a film negative, they look as barren as volcanic eruptions. But as we draw nearer the coastline the colors develop. A stubble of olive trees clutch into the red earth; the sun glitters on remotely scattered buildings—square blocks of salt, set into the wooded hillsides. There is no grouping of houses that would suggest a town, or even a village.

"If you ever go to Ibiza," Cynthia had said to me, never supposing that I would have either the money or the enterprise to do so—and very naturally cherishing the exclusiveness that could not be spoiled by realistic comparison—"you will be surprised how the capital and port of the island is suddenly upon you. One moment you will be following a range of endless mountains, and the next, after rounding a point where a lighthouse stands, you will be in the harbor and looking up to a town whose houses cling like sea gulls to the sides of a pointed hill, and crowned by a fortress and citadel that circle the cathedral."

I had discovered even at this advanced stage of her self-imposed austerity that there was a vein of soft white chalkiness not very far below the surface that acted as an alkali on her increasingly acid nature; that sometimes the most cynical observations could be diverted into the soft flapping of a dove's wings. It was easy to bring tears to her large eyes, but it must be for a sufficiently small reason, like a childish effort thwarted. Real disaster simply hardened her; in most cases she considered it was well deserved.

Now, as Stephen and I stand at the rails of the ship becoming accustomed to, and a little bored by, the unchanging coast line, I wonder if the headland and lighthouse do really exist, or whether they too may have been a pinnacle of retreat from the hard work and poverty of the West Kensington flat— whether the white houses clinging to the hill were only shallow pulses that beat in sudden creative ecstasy within the delicate hollows of her small skull.

We walk to the stern of the ship and look back at the foaming peacock's tail we leave behind, at what is passing rather than what is to come. Suddenly Stephen says: "Let's go to the front again. I think the course has changed. Did you feel it?"

❖   ❖   ❖

Jasper was onto me about my eye before we had known each other three months. His approach was tactful but adamant: "You simply must have it done; apart from what it looks like, it's bad for you to feel that you're different from other girls."

I thought, he is a perfectionist and it is his way of saying that he wishes his possessions to be flawless. I read into the gentle coaxing subtleties that went far beyond the limited feelings that one human being can have for another. When he said, "I want to pay for you to have it done comfortably, Hatty," I accepted it as a bridal veil. So, one dark November evening I found myself in a room leading off one of the centrally heated tunnels of the Middlesex Hospital.

He came to see me the day after the operation. I lay in a white iron bedstead, one eye covered and the other weakly watering in sympathy, and I tried to feel the moisture of reciprocated love in the papery dryness of his lined hand.

There was a second spring before the first threat of winter coldness in the relationship.

Up until that moment, except within the secrecy of my own interior monologues, I had been unable to bring myself to ever openly call him by his Christian name; I would hesitate when about to address an envelope and then with a bravado that was tingling with self-conscious uncertainty write the name "Jasper" rather more heavily than the "Lomax."

We lay one afternoon dozing on the top of his day bed in the large furnished room he rented when he was in London, just off the Earls Court Road.

"I notice, Hatty," he said softly into my ear, "that you have never called me by my Christian name; and although I think I can guess the reason for this, don't you think 'Jassy' would be a little less impersonal now and then?"

This, I remember, was a shock; it made me immediately self-conscious both for his sake as well as for my own. It made me raise myself on my elbow and pull at the rumpled skirt of my dress and drag it further down over my bare knees. All at once it became imperative that I should stand up and be at an advantage. Before I rolled off the bed I noticed with cold detachment the corrugation of lines that ran like puckered stitching across his forehead, the pronounced widow's peak that I could now see was accentuated with the razor. I began to hate him for his turkey's neck and protruding Adam's apple.

But he was ahead of me, sensitive as a professional diviner; he too, was on his feet, stretching his arms above his head; he filled in the square of window space with the width of his great muscled shoulders.

Then going to the chest of drawers, he pulled out a bright blue spotted scarf and looped it casually, but with perfect precision, round his neck in sailor fashion. I was swept back into the deep water; now well beyond the depth when it would be possible to put foot to ground. "Darling," I said muzzily, "I'll call you anything you like, or perhaps just 'darling' forever."

I gave too much, unknowingly, yet I was pleased with myself for the generosity and the sound of the term of affection so fresh on my lips. But the crafty teddy bear who had wound the spring up to go so far, and no further, became suddenly wary, perhaps shocked at the giving. "Come on," he said smiling down at me from the summit of his full age, holding a surprise for the child behind his back, "let's go gay, a little music and some dinner in Soho, with a bottle of Rosé d'Anjou."

It was after that, some time between the stunted summer and prolonged autumn that I began knowingly to deceive myself. I still visited my uncle and his wife, now more and more for the reason of bringing to life something I knew to be fading in front of my eyes. I spoke to Cynthia on all occasions when there was doubt in my mind; like a moth I went straight toward the flame that would destroy me, listening with rapt attention to the words and tiny shafts that fell from her lips. Sometimes she seemed to torment me, but she would not let me die.

"He would be a fool to miss the chance of marrying you," she would say, bringing to birth the thin fantasy that could hardly survive on its own within me. Later I was to discover that this was only a cue for me to commit myself still further, adding to the already growing heap of indiscretions and follies.

"Do you think that perhaps he doesn't say anything because of the difference in our ages?" I had asked her once as I sat in her drawing room, dazed by the warmth of her sympathy and the flickering jets of the gas fire. Now, it was in this very room that I actually lived through the motions of my romantic phases with Jasper relying on Cynthia to extend the possibilities of the future by sustaining the actualities of the past.

Cynthia had her own difficulties. My uncle, now finally retired from his staff job, found himself the recipient of a shrunken income that was the disability pension of a retired lieutenant-colonel. Unbeknown to him, she now put her child in a state day nursery and went out in the mornings to work in the houses of other people, sweeping and dusting. Yet she was always in and installed by the fire with the boy by the time he came in from his club after tea. So she supplemented their income; and he, not knowing of the little inflow of money, thought her a miracle maker and loved her the more for it. All this I knew, and I found it hard to accept. If it had been in conjunction with anyone else but my uncle I should have seen it in the true light of heroism; as it was she was overshadowed, blighted. She both infected and was affected by him; as his temples narrowed and he squared his jaw in disapproval of me, so I repulsed them both, and dug my feet more firmly into the awful certainty of the shifting sands.

The island is like everything of picture-book quality that I have always wished to believe in: the mysterious paths leading through planes of extraordinary happiness to security off the page, the most powerful safety valve of escape to the childish eye. Now the richness of color and texture are here beneath my hands and feet; yet it is not the fresh greenness of England that is so quickly drained away from one's vision, leaving a tattering of rags on the stick branches, nor the first pale flutter of yellow that follows so slowly yet so temporarily. Here everything is thicker, deeper, and more sustained. The loud pedal full on and never the foot raised. There is no intermediary season, no bareness, no rags.

The village of Santa Eulalia, ten kilometers west of the port, takes us two hours to reach. Our hotel proprietor, who is at the landing stage to meet us in a battered car, drives to the market place of the town; then *"Un momento,"* he says, slipping from the seat, and leaves us for more than sixty minutes in the deepening glare.

At first we look every five minutes at the clock on the dashboard; then we lie back in resignation against the dusty sour-smelling upholstery, the impatience fading away into the sun. Who does time belong to, I begin to wonder, that we should barter over the minutes under this clear blue sky?

The entrance to the village is as sudden as the approach to the port has been. After driving along straight roads, poplar-lined, leading to nowhere, there is an ancient low arched bridge; a shallow flowing river below has smoothed the brown homely rocks to a domestic comfort. Growing thickly at the water's edge, and even over the width of the river on the larger stones whose hollows have been silted with a thin layer of mud, blooms the wild pinkness of the oleander: the flower that Cynthia carried in her mind all those hard years in the felted depths of Stamford Gardens.

Trailing banks of giant blue convolvulus, purple

bougainvillea twisted into the formal intricacy of black wrought iron—all hang downward toward the sea. Lemons in the hotel garden, still green but ripening in patches, and below the shelving gardens, the wilder unfenced land parceled into small plots, sloping away to the sea's edge: everywhere the stunted gray of the olive trees. With our small rationed vision we are like greedy children looking everywhere for more and more; we stare into the brilliance like seers, seeking an unsimple and deeper quality; when we do not find it, we call it surfeit.

In the heat of the siesta we lie panting for breath on the narrow beds, hardly longer than cots; the first meal in the hotel has been entirely yellow: fried eggs on a bank of saffron-colored rice, and yellow plums whose unripe flesh still clung to the stone.

"Do you think we shall be able to come to grips with all this beauty and leisure?" I ask Stephen. "I wish I could find a piano in the village."

"Why don't you take the opportunity of soaking up the brandy at threepence a glass?" he answers me from where he floats beneath the first layers of a deepening sleep.

After a few days, I find myself watching for the post to come and bring letters from Hampstead and Bloomsbury. When there is nothing, there is a terrible finality about it, for there are only three posts a week.

One day Amy writes in her square-nibbed script: "I ordered a white sheaf for Cynthia from you; carnations filled in with white lilac and gypsophila."

After the first six months of our knowing each other, I found it impossible to carry within my mind a clear picture of myself in relation to Jasper. My vision was blurred, because I had outwardly accepted the state. I would have noticed nothing except drastic change or sudden removal. Small things began to gain significance. The fact that he would run at my side without the audible breathing that I associated with age made me eulogize extravagantly: "You must have been a cross-country runner; really darling, you're like an Achilles." And from thence developed the joke motion that we called secretly "the Achilles hop"—a long-legged stride that took us on springy legs to bus stop and underground station, causing my heart to beat with a steady excitement.

With Cynthia, though, there was clarity and discernment. Many times she would stress, unmercifully I thought, the thinness of his neck, the permanent droop of his shoulders, and the thick yellowing of his gray thatch that he took such pains to dress, peering (as I had often seen him do) into his three-sided looking glass to get a good view of the back. All these things, superimposed by Cynthia over the real picture, I stored up and chose privately to magnify for his belittlement, as if by doing so I ensured a personal detachment. In her way Cynthia helped me to stay the process of advancement; perhaps also she prolonged the pain.

I found, too, that I had an ally in Ted. "You're becoming quite a popsy," he told me, "with those whirlpool eyes and all that paint on your face." It was now quite simple to go out with him and lay aside the gnawing anxiety of whether one could think of anything to say that would not be overridden or dissected into minute particles of stupidity.

I had practically abandoned my piano at home; sometimes I strummed for the pleasure of my aunt and uncle. Jasper was almost completely tone deaf, but I did not judge him for it. Instead I kept my talent that he could not share well in abeyance, bringing it out only occasionally when he was not there.

Ted heard me play the Beethoven Appassionata one day at Cynthia's, and said, "You have passion and style, Hatty; sometimes you play like a great artist, and sometimes like a halfwit with no coordination or understanding."

I accepted his assessment because it was valid; even, it seemed, the words of praise. It was possible to accept the full truth of half artist or genius *manqué* now that it no longer mattered.

Jasper had a house on the edge of the Essex marshes. A rambling whitewashed farmstead surrounded by chestnut palings, it stood in a jungle of cultivated disorderliness. Coarse salt-tipped grass grew at the edge of the paths and giant poppies that had seeded themselves into the suffocating undergrowth of St. John's wort and bindweed. The garden sank into a hollow where there was shelter from the North Sea winds.

Here on a bed of wild roses and convolvulus suckers, we would sit and look out across the course of the flat brown river whose level sank so low in the summer drought. It reminded him of India, he said; and although I had been born there I wished he would not tell me that there was anywhere else on earth that could compare with this private paradise.

I wondered sometimes if perhaps he might have ever contracted a marriage with a Eurasian, and that this was the reason for his silence. My grandfathers on both sides had done this, though until the advent of Ted I had always been led to believe that their brides had been a Sicilian and a Spaniard of noble birth. "Haven't you seen the bridal photographs in Otway's album, my dear? They're as black as your hat."

I could not even bring myself to expose this fact to Jasper; it was too near the bone. He had given me my eye, and for this I would never be able to repay him.

He must have felt the weight and pressure of my unasked questions; because of them I found very little else to say.

One day in the garden, he suggested that it would be a good thing if I joined a club for young people. "Cynthia's son should be able to help you over that," he said, "although I've always suspected the fellow of being a little Red, and we don't want you mixed up with Bolshies, do we, Hatty?" I saw fit in a moment of temper to bring out some of the catchphrases of Ted's that had lodged at the back of my mind without use until just such an occasion; the clarity of his suggestion caused me to lash about me with these blunted weapons of whose strength I had no idea.

Now there was misunderstanding at all levels.

On the train to London we hardly spoke a word; dry-eyed and cold with apprehension, we parted at Liverpool Street station, no word, no renewal of faith, nothing.

So it was winter again, and the time passing with an existence eked out on so few meetings that they could no longer be called consecutive. I knew that even in conversation I could not say: "I see Jasper now and then," but rather: "I don't see Jasper very often now."

One afternoon I remember particularly. It had been an iron-hard January, the gas pressure so low that I walked about the house in fur boots to keep my feet warm. I still continued the painful operation of telephoning to keep the contact alive, even at widely spaced intervals; in this I was influenced unconsciously by Cynthia and her long patience with my uncle before they married. "If you want something enough, there is nothing that can stop you getting it except yourself," she had once said.

I went to the telephone and spoke to Jasper. "You must come to dinner tonight," I said. "I've got something very special, a bottle of Imperial Tokay, and this is just the day to drink it," I added with the kind of reckless humor that is born on the wings of hysteria.

Afterward, as I went about the task of preparing the meal, I felt all the apprehension and strain it had cost me to make the call after a three weeks' silence.

When he arrived, he was blue with cold; it seemed

I could do nothing to produce warmth. He kept his muffler on all through dinner, and I watched the food grow thick as white jade on our plates between each mouthful. Even the precious wine had no fire in it, and remained dead and frosted in the glasses.

I think he felt for me then, in my ugly and exposed dilemma; as he sat on the sofa, rubbing his hands in a perpetual washing movement, his stiff winged collar made me think of an elderly solicitor, a commissioner for oaths, a close friend of the family.

"My dear," he had said as he was going, "fond as I am of you, I can't have you spending all your hard-earned pennies on me."

"You see how it was?" I say to Stephen one morning after breakfast when we were sitting out above the beach on the spongy bank of sea dross, brindled as a hedgehog's back, that fringes the whole island between the fields and the sea. "I had to go on telling Cynthia everything; there was simply no one else. Mother had gone to live with Great-aunt in Salisbury, and anyway there wasn't much understanding between us since I'd had my eye done. You know, she never once said she was pleased or that she noticed the difference."

"She was probably irritated that she hadn't been

able to pay for it herself, that's nearer the truth," Stephen answers, dispelling the cobwebs of resentment that could spin themselves across the lightness of the sky. Now as he lies beside me in the full blaze of the sun it seems to me that for the first time in his life he too is worming his way out of the chrysalis; his blue trunks expose a scar below the navel that is still a livid red, unlike the golden brown on the rest of his body. He once told me that it was the beginning of a rupture he got in the army from unloading a heavy truck; but I feel that it is a late snapping of the umbilical cord.

I pull my big-brimmed hat further over my face; I cannot really afford to let the lines at the corners of my eyes become too pronounced. It is strange to think of the mild effort I make now to preserve the smoothness of my skin, that before I had regarded as only a blankness of countenance. The balance is completely reversed; and with this new contentment I can afford the generosity of recollection. If I went to see Jasper today, he might be quite pleased to see me, I think. Poor Jasper in his Sydenham boarding house, riddled with arthritis. Why did he never marry anyone, I wonder? Perhaps he really hated women in a permanent relationship except as sisters or mothers.

Stephen is now deeply asleep; the thickness of his

heavy lids screens him from the glare that exposes to me every plane and crevice of his dark face. How strange has been the reassembling and solution of our lives; Cynthia newly dead, myself newly married, Jasper a resigned invalid. The pain and the urgency had gone forever. Did nobody love anyone in those days, or only themselves? Was it all an illusion of youth?

We find the time lapse between breakfast and lunch at three o'clock a great discipline. We go from extremes of hunger to complete indifference about food; and, as this takes place, our stomachs shrink, so that when the time comes we pick like birds at the food before us.

Today there is a whole pile of letters and papers for us. We fall upon them like wild animals and take them into the dining room with us.

There is a letter for me from Ted. We have always remained friendly and he never took sides in the trouble between his mother and myself. Once, in the war, he made me an offer. "Not exactly marriage, because as you know I don't hold with such medieval conceptions, but we would make a unit, set up in rooms somewhere—a revolutionary monogamy. You could pay half the rent," he had said.

Today his letter, three closely written pages, is

full of description and ironic humor; a transparent
covering over the gap caused by his mother's death:

> ...*All the family, including your mother,
> turned up in black crêpe and veils. You should
> have seen them pushing for the best place in the
> churchyard. There was quite a little incident
> at one moment when the undertakers had to
> drive them back from the crumbling raw earth.*
>
> *Step-Pa, very upright and soldierly. The
> tears he shed were small and steely. I felt like
> a midget beside him—also I was the only mem-
> ber of the party in tweeds.*
>
> *I noticed Jasper during the proceedings
> standing very much apart from the rest of us,
> very tottery on two sticks. And now Hatty, here
> is* an occurrence *for you, something spooky to
> give you the creeps under all that Mediter-
> ranean blue.*
>
> *I traveled back, when it was all over, in a
> car with your mother. She was most sympa-
> thetic to me in her best cut-glass manners until
> I mentioned quite chattily that I'd no idea
> Jasper was such a wreck. Then she rounded on
> me as if I'd used a dirty word: "Edward," she
> said, "Major Lomax was* not *at the funeral. He*

no doubt would have wished to be there. But he is completely bedridden now and hasn't been able to leave his room for over a year." I was just going to say, "O.K. so you think I'm tight, but I saw him with my own eyes," when she gave me a freezing look and shut down with "Major Lomax sent the sheaf of red roses that went down into the earth with her. The undertakers mistook it for Otway's, but he thought it wise to say nothing."

What a fearful thing. I checked up later and found out that your mother was quite right about Jasper. Do you think I'm going off my chump?

At the luncheon table I am not eager to read out this letter of Ted's; there is a kind of resistance to him in Stephen, a lack of sympathy that springs from a dislike of what he might have been, rather than what he actually is. I slip my letter under the pile of newspapers. It is a long detour, but how strong and detached one can be in one's deceit, what resistance, and what capitulation finally.

Cynthia said to me one day as I looked out over her back garden that was covered with a layer of leaf mold, "Jasper is exceedingly fond of you; he is really worried about your future."

That was the moment that I began to gyrate and spin like a hysterical top, and then to hate in a clearly defined and motionless way. Why had she said this to me now of all times, I asked myself? Someone must have prompted her, and who else but Jasper himself? They were meeting together, I thought, forming a cabal against me, planning my future, and I was as isolated from it all as if I had been inside a barrel studded with nails waiting to be pushed off into the void. As I listened to her continuing voice, there was the thin squawk of a one-seasoned bird from the branch of a bare tree; it had not learned that by repetition only can one know when it is not expedient to make the voice heard.

There was another false start before the bitter end.

The telephone rang one morning during the Easter holidays. "I've decided to leave Number Twenty-four and take a flat in a house I used to know in Cadogan Gardens. Come and have a day at Heal's, Hatty, and help me choose things to put in it."

The sun was terrific at that moment, golden and soft, lighting up every corner and doubt in my mind. I could afford, in spite of the terrible silences when I had thought the tide finally on the wane, to say: "How lovely, but I don't think I can manage it today, I've promised to go with Ted to an opening at the Leicester Galleries."

Jasper was irritated, his voice all at once squeaky like an excited parrot. "Can't you put him off for another day? After all, it isn't often that I ask you to do anything for me."

It was the willful desire to please, rather than the knowledge of sustaining uncertainty, that made me ring off and then go back on my self-preserving lie when I telephoned him ten minutes later.

What a day! Light airy rooms, unlived-in, slung like great hammocks above the seething traffic of the Tottenham Court Road, visited continually by human beings in pairs. Couples were drawn into the shop, magnetized by the artificial hominess that they were searching for. Now for a second their vision was clear and unimpaired—so this is what a home is like—our home—as if a glimpse of eternity had been revealed to them, then quickly wiped away. For ultimately it is only the absence of things in a room that we notice; daily acceptance blunts the sensibilities as surfeit clogs the imagination.

Jasper said, fitting his long back into a low chair like a hollowed-out tree trunk: "Isn't this contemporary stuff restful? And the space it saves! How do you like the bleached pine of that table? Perhaps I shall get you to wax it for me one day."

Into this well-equipped impermanence I was already deeply dreaming. I was letting myself out of a house on the edge of a leafy square; there was yellow pollen from the red-tailed willows sprinkled over the sun-soaked pavement. . . .

I was afraid to say when it was all over: "This has been one of the happiest days of my life." I walked home lighted up with hope without even space for the anxiety and question of when we should meet again.

Cynthia said with a brilliant sharpness, when she heard of the expedition, "Well, this is certainly a change. I've never heard Jasper express the desire to have a home in London too; perhaps he's simply sick of lodgings and wants to do his own cooking."

After the three o'clock luncheon the heat steps up and it is impossible to go out; the whole village retires until the sun has left off raging in the middle of the bay and begun its westward trail up beyond the long chain of mountains behind which it will finally disappear.

Today we sit out on the hotel verandah under an

awning of dried bamboo stalks; they are hollow like the pipes of an organ, always filled with the sounds of twittering birds. The inhabitants call this island the White Island of Nightingales. In the spring months of February and March a cloud of almond blossom settles over the shallow orchards; there is a nightingale for every tree they say. In this early summertime we hear only the dry clicking of the cricket, and at nighttime the regular shrill squawk of a tethered jackass.

The stunted bell-hung farm creatures move slowly in the fields as they must have done in biblical times; there has been little change in the methods of farming, the banked-up channels for irrigating the fields are as ancient as the river that feeds them. I have noticed that it is the women who work the longest hours in the fields; the married women in their black dresses shaded by rough straw hats fastened under the chin look like Red Indian squaws with their braids swinging over their shoulders. They are sturdier than the men, more heavily built, less compromising in their austerity; their waists do not dip under the brilliant support of a cummerbund or spiked leather belt. On Sundays only they change their attire, and swarm up to the twelfth-century church on the mountainside in their layers of thick skirts, heads covered by a dull brown shawl fringed and tasseled, while the shorter pieces of hair are plastered into stiff little curls on brow and cheek.

Here time has no significance except in its capacity to link birth to death. Lives are held cheaply in the eyes of the islanders, and this is partly because of a deep-seated acceptance of spiritual values, and partly because the effort to survive is very great. Children are cherished and protected with ferociousness until they are able to stand on their own feet; they grow quickly to maturity, and after that there is no sign of the prolonged infantilism so common in our colder islands.

Suddenly we are surprised to see two strangers; a man and a woman climb the steep flight of steps from the road to the hotel terrace. There is something in their movements that suggests that they are English before we actually hear them speak. They go to the far end of the verandah and order something to drink. Through half-closed lids, we regard each other like trespassing cats. We hear their voices, smooth and well cared for as the doors of the reclaimed terraces in Chelsea or South Kensington. It is impossible to bridge the silence; the temptation is extreme, but the effort out of all proportion. I look at this golden woman and think that she is like a full-blown moss rose; complete in her species, she has survived without the dexterity of wood grafting. The man is low-toned, neutral; perhaps he is an official from the consulate on the mainland.

"If we have enough money left," Stephen says, to draw my attention away from the visitors, "I'll take you for a trip to the islet of Formenterra." His pencil hovers over the map and he punctures the paper into the blue sea about three miles off the coast of Ibiza. I feel this diversion as a stroke of technique to make me look away from the couple. The thought is obsessive and unreasonable. Why should I interpret this to be more than husbandly thoughtfulness? I am as well preserved as the woman at the other end of the verandah, I do not feel my years; yet somewhere hidden not very far beneath the skin is the puckered scar of my corrected eye.

I hear a sentence drift across from them: "A middle-aged bridal pair." Nothing more. It is applicable to us, but it could not be a criticism unless we are stamped with the mark of our one-year's marriage.

Stephen has dropped the map and withdrawn into himself. How far apart we are, sitting together side by side. I know that it is not enough simply to coordinate two lives by the trick of words and vows; rarely spaced are the moments that two people can settle together on a pinnacle of illumination or understanding and count it as unity. I thought always before the operation on my eye that the source of discordancy between myself and other people lay in the distortion of my own vision; I did not know then as I do now that this outward sign was only the visible proof of inward impediment.

Now in the cool of late afternoon, the pink clouds of dust that were disturbed by the cartwheels settle once more in the solid terracotta ground. We go down to the beach again, picking our way along the narrow streak of path between the floppy bamboo trees and bits of farmyard that have never coordinated into a whole, yet manage to supply the hotel and its visitors with milk, eggs, and fruit.

The water is shallow where we bathe, and never comes above the waist. Here the river flows into the sea and the land on either side of the estuary flattens out as it opens its arms. Always when I bathe from this beach, after the first few strokes out, I turn and look inland toward the mountains; from this distance they are dense and mysterious (probably only a few hundred feet above sea level) yet as remote to me as if they were shrouded in the obscurity of clouds. Shallow infiltration of the foothills has revealed that it is the spiked greenery of conifers and rosemary scrub that turns to black when distance drains the color away.

"We'll try and climb one of the mountains tomorrow when it's cool." Stephen's voice blows landward, striking for an instant against the clump of silver-barked trees, strung together like a lyre, before it is flung back to me. I am thinking all the time of the significance of mountains, how there has always been pain and discovery in every ascent from Table to Golgotha, that the Seven Final Words of illumination were as baffling and catastrophic as The Death itself.

Coming out of the water, I have a clear picture of Cynthia on just such an afternoon, picking her way with care through the strip of stone-scattered mud to the beach: poor little legs—now brittle and stiff as twigs.

Stephen, who has a talent for catching unspoken words and running them together like dropped stitches along a needle, says: "I think you should try not to brood so much on the ghoulish details of Cynthia's death and burial. You have nothing to reproach yourself with, and it isn't even important now to know the exact reason for her bitterness. You must accept that it is impossible for you to ever divorce the facts of reality from imaginative interpretation; they have become too much entwined."

Now he has hit the nail accurately on the head and the shock sets going a whole mechanism. I run swiftly up toward the trees where we have left our pile of clothes, a gathering knot of resentment for this detached assessment. How can he speak of who was right and who was wrong, even by deed of thought? "Rats in their traps have at least the limitation of their own ineffectuality," I say heatedly, as I worm into my cotton dress, "and anyway you can hardly know about something that happened when you could barely walk."

I still cannot accept the truth of his complete affection; I try to search all the time for reasons that are too obviously humble, and at the same time over-arrogant. I have never seen myself except in the reflection of another person's eyes; today I have no idea who I am.

"One day it will all fit together," says Stephen unperturbed, "and then you will see and be able to accept the past for what it was. You must go on the fact that Cynthia at the time of the trouble was all for maintaining a family front; she wanted above all to stop the crumbling; and that was what Jasper was in effect, a well-meaning irresponsible crumbler."

Jasper a crumbler. At that time, already the clouds
were beginning to build up behind Cynthia. I saw her
as an all-powerful magician who could produce black
evil and despair at the flick of her wrist. Her small
white voice creaked on, in and out of the teacups as
she sat smiling at me behind the tray; these were no
longer objects of domestic comfort, but stark recep-
tacles for surgical performance, something in which
to catch the sly tear, or conceal for a second, with
the raising of a hand, the buttoned-down anguish of
the mouth.

"There's no shame attached to it, Hatty dear," she
had said to me. "I doubt now if Jasper ever gives any
woman a second glance. I'll tell you an enlightening
story one of these days. Anyway, have a heart; he's
old enough to be your father."

My father. That was perhaps the simple answer to
the situation. My own father had had a strong will
and the brutality to lay waste any small efforts of
survival that did not amount to complete independence. Cynthia was suggesting to me that Jasper was
the counterpart to this mythical figure, who had died
before I had had time to discover if he existed at all.
My mother shielded his memory in every way she
knew; his likeness was enshrined in the silver frame
which she kept always beside her bed. I could only

assess it by the living resemblance in the thin down-turned lips of my uncle Otway; I knew the brothers had been very close.

I wished desperately that I had not exposed so much of my thoughts to Cynthia. I tried vainly to create a fog of deception with small lies and false trails, but they did not adhere to the bald patches.

Jasper's going from my day-to-day life gave now to the seasons and places which we had shared together another dimension. What had radiated from its vegetation and stonework a golden happiness, now absorbed all the light and gave back only an acid sense of revelation that ate into the bone as it continued to reveal.

They were all meeting together. My uncle, his wife, and their old friend. They were talking and explaining; wiping away the laughable misunderstanding that had grown up as a result of "the trouble over Hatty." The summer days and hopes of spring were washed away. Everything that had ever been said between us transposed to a well-modulated and acceptable convention.

"I think a great deal of her. Her wit; and she's so talented in many ways. I admit, Cynthia, that I've been a damned old fool, but I couldn't be more sorry if I've really upset the apple cart." Cynthia had a talent for mimicry. She could report conversations with the exact inflection and tone that left no doubt, no saving grace. She was as heartless as a tape recorder.

Soon after that I had made my decision. The last thing I remember her saying, leaving me not a rag, not a thread of comfort to wrap myself in, was: "I'm afraid life's like that; you'll have to learn to take it as it comes."

She struggled, God alone knows how she struggled, under the heavy weight of her iron will. My withdrawal from her orbit was something she had not bargained for. She went on trying, even when they had moved to the country, but I pecked and fenced and finally I knew one day for certain that her voice on the telephone would never reach me again. I killed her voice gradually; at first it would not die but bounced up time after time like a rubber ball.

"What is so odd," Stephen says, while we are drinking our breakfast cup of tea, poured from a shiny brown pot inscribed "Té Lipton," and eating the dry vanilla buns, "what is so odd to me is that in the end there was practically nothing left of the Cynthia you first described as a young woman, nothing of the creature who worked and loafed in these islands. She was completely made over by the marriage to your uncle; for that reason you should have been able to forgive her."

As he is speaking I can see clearly the posed photograph that stood always on my uncle's grand piano: a timeless drapery of net framed the bare shoulders, striking a diagonal line below the small pointed chin—so frailly visible beneath the white stretched skin, her small-boned face was as delicately exposed as a wren's carcass. She looked out over the pretty room which she had created, like a stranger who had arrived somewhere by chance and sought nothing more than to be remembered as she was when the camera had caught her in that split second.

"I don't know why people have their photographs taken," I say. "Cynthia altered so much in her appearance that strangers used to ask who it was in the place of honor on the piano. She used to laugh; obviously she got a kick in keeping the record of the person she had once been always before her eyes."

"It must have been her peak period," Stephen smiles. "People sometimes go through their whole lives without ever reaching the moment when they are exactly the person they want to be."

As he talks away, building upward and outward like a sleepy child with bricks, I think about the hidden talent or uniqueness of character that lies sealed within most of us; how it is like the work of a sculptor who sees within a block of marble a trapped masterpiece and must chip and grind until it is released. "She certainly chose a hard way," he continues. "The martyr's streak is what was strongest in her, that's quite obvious."

The boy Antonio is early today with the post. Hardly are we back from the beach when he comes swinging up the steps of the hotel toward us, on his arm the flat straw basket that he has not yet had time to examine. We hold ourselves in this time; when he has passed through the wire-netted doors of the house and stopped at the empty bar that he uses as a sorting table, we shall saunter in and first order a drink to put off the delightful moment.

I watch his broad sunburned hands that are covered with clusters of grapelike warts; some he has treated with acid, and the treatment has left small patches of weeping flesh that I find particularly sickening when he handles the dishes of under-cooked goat.

"*Pas de lettres*," he turns to the funny expectant foreigners who have tried so hard to conceal their eagerness; he smiles and shrugs his shoulders sympathetically, then disappears through the kitchen doors to prepare the *citron pressé* we have ordered to neutralize our disappointment.

What can one do with beauty after the eye of the camera has clicked? It is eight days since we arrived and as yet I can invest no emotional quality to the brilliant unblinking panorama beyond the window. It is as unreal as celluloid, until I actually bend down and scratch my fingers on a thorn of cactus. One must find fertile soil in the imagination in which to send down roots; nothing can be taken for granted until it is credibly set off against a familiar theme. This is the paradox of age and reason. In childhood it is different; there are flexibilities and infinite potentialities; then one can accept the authenticity of the unfamiliar with unclouded innocence and grapple to oneself the rounded and the shining, like bright toys; then quickly begin the cocoon of tradition.

It is within the vacuum of "No letters from England" that I begin to fray away at the foreign brilliance. Each day we have regarded the siesta as a time for gently inhaling the fumes of the fiery brandy we have just swallowed to wipe away the taste of the bad coffee. Tight across the window of our room the mosquito netting casts a lattice over the bay; below, on the bleached road, nothing stirs but the slowly rising and falling dust from the wheels of an isolated farm cart on its way. The patches of fields banding the sea's edge are empty except for a tethered goat drowsing on its haunches. The hotel proprietor and his family are having their luncheon on the verandah; their voices filter up toward us through the bamboo roof. Everyone is resting, waiting for the sun to bloom like an enormous peony far up behind the dark range of hills so that work and life may begin again.

Stephen is ahead of me in sleep; with casual ease he has folded himself into the narrow iron cot against the other wall.

There is something in the simple outline of the iron bed frame against the whitewashed walls that soothes and touches me; in such a bed for the first ten years of my life I had been hemmed in, vision limited at night by the straight black railings. This afternoon it is only a trick on the borders of sleep that gives me the power to develop within myself the exact angle of a blistered shutter, listen intently to hear again the sound of cloth-slippered feet over village cobbles, smell again authentically the hot afternoon geraniums and mimosa that overflow the beds below in this abbey garden in South Brittany.

If I had not met Stephen for the first time in this very garden, I do not think that I would have listened and heard anything; I do not think that I would have been able to bridge the difficulties of the years that separated us, not so long after I had decided on my own solitary course.

I went back for the first time since my girlhood to St.-Polignac-sur-Mer in the Morbihan, after the war. It was the August of 1954.

To go back to the past on this occasion was like to the slow process of befogging the present and dulling the future. To enter again into these stilled places made stagnant by the years and perhaps fed by only a trickle of underground memory was to push heavy-limbed through the water, thick with deadly weeds, yet covered over with innocent surface flowers. They say that death by drowning is the least violent of ends—gradual enveloping, the roar of the water like pipe music fills the apertures of the skull. It is the bringing back to life that is more terrible, the frantic revival of the victims who are dragged out of the duckweed too soon and pounded and pummeled mercilessly back into life.

I walked back into this fabric of my extreme youth and early adolescence, and the complex of hopes and despairs was still there, preserved like a stillborn fetus, in the garden and cloisters of this ancient building that I had known since birth. From the long polished corridors and in the shuttered music room, I could still hear quite clearly the sounds of my own practicing; trilling and pounding away into the brilliant future I had been so certain of then.

I had got down from the bus at the Post Office Square and walked along the village street; the figures who stood at their cottage doors were many of them the same; ageless people dyed to the color of ripe chestnuts by the sun and salt winds. Those that recognized me came over their stone steps and took my hand in their horny palms: "*Ah, mais vous n'avez pas changé, Mademoiselle 'atty. C'est bien vous.*" No one referred to the changes in my appearance, nor the fact that my right eye no longer turned inward.

The effect of the walk was belittling, stripping me of my thirty-seven years. When I came down to dinner that night into the enormous crowd that gathered in the *salle à manger*, I felt rudderless, acutely conscious that I had not my mother to say: "Sit here, Hatty; and you'd better not have the *tomates farcies*, as it's made of twice-cooked meat."

Rushes of cool air circulating the length of the big room, from the doors open at each end, lifted the edges of my cotton dress, billowing into the full sleeves, filling them with emptiness. I walked cautiously between the damask-covered tables forested

with wine bottles, under the fixed gaze of the enormous plaster saints in their brilliant robes who stood
on pedestals just above the heads of the seated
visitors.

I was directed to a table for four people. Hardly
was I seated when the muscled forearm of a village
serving girl, with the first dish of the meal balanced
on her hip, came round to the left of my head, and I
was reaching up and helping myself for the first
time. I wondered whether I should order wine; it
was the custom, but I had never been offered it in
the past; perhaps it would go to my head and I
should be unable to get up from my chair at the end
of the meal.

There were two French women sitting in the
chairs opposite me; they looked like schoolteachers.
They unrolled their table napkins from the pewter
rings with practiced brown fingers; they reached out
easily with a certain sun-soaked languor toward the
stack of wine bottles on our table and discovered
their own. They were dressed for dinner in white; the
newly starched collars glittered like chalk against
the dense mahogany of their seamed throats. We
bowed ceremoniously to one another: "*Madame . . .*"
and I asked for the salt.

"*Vous êtes ici depuis longtemps, Madame?*"

Tentatively I unrolled the forgotten language, slipping a little on the last syllable.

"*Depuis un mois, Madame, nous venons de Paris toutes les années depuis la guerre. Les champs et les plages de St.-Polignac nous paraissent délicieux....*"

They spoke as if to reveal to me something about the place that I should not know. But I understood them now beyond their words. The fetish of the health seeker who lives most of the year in the city; the curiously obsessive expanse of the pure white and well-tended teeth in their middle-aged skulls that might become in a thousand years as exciting and rare as the ivory tusks of some now extinct species. I envied for a moment the pure concentration and purpose that these women applied to everything, whether they were lecturing at their *lycée* or absorbing good health at a fishing village.

A hand fell on the back of the empty chair beside me—a set of tapering fingers that were as boneless as a girl's, yet the flat cushions between the finger joints were tufted with a dark hair that had much of the quality of lichen. The fingers curled themselves round the yellow wood and the chair scraped outward.

My eyes moved instinctively away from the newcomer; over the far edge of the table and out into the sea of unknown faces I searched as if this was a considered movement rather than one of escape. When I looked back at my empty plate, I saw that the French ladies were beaming across the table to the place beside me: *"Eh bien, Monsieur, vous avez pris une bonne pêche?"* I turned to smile now in accordance with the convention, as if I had just arrived.

The newcomer ate with fantastic speed, making up for lost time. He had soon caught up with the rest of us; he answered falteringly between mouthfuls: *"Pas des homards, Madame, mais beaucoup de shrimps."*

I was eased by the familiarity of his words; they touched off a hidden spring bringing suddenly to light afternoons spent in the scorching sun with the white rope of shrimping nets sagging in deep rock pools dark with seaweed, and all around from out of damp crevices of the rocks the clicking of lobsters who watched unseen.

"There used to be an Englishwoman staying here once who knew the secret of the lobster hideouts," I said. "She never came back from the islands without at least two, and a huge spider crab as well sometimes."

One of the serving girls approached the table carrying a big tureen filled with newly boiled shrimps; they were threaded with the fine hairs of cooked seaweed. The man laughed as they were placed in front of him.

"And I," he turned now directly to me, "was equally optimistic and blind once in a London club. I ordered hot lobster, only to discover too late that the smudged writing on the menu concealed the minced up remains of yesterday's joint in what they tactfully described as Homemade Pie!"

I noticed, now that he faced me, that his widely spaced eyes were splashed with yellow like the points of agate in a tabby cat's eyes; the wiry tendrils of hair, dark as a jackdaw's wing, had been bleached and split at the ends by the sun and the salt water.

The red wine that I had finally ordered I found rough and astringent to my palate; but it was surprising to discover the power within oneself to manipulate so easily the long thin neck of the bottle and tip it toward the tumbler without spilling any onto the tablecloth.

I got up quickly when I had finished, not wishing to test the moment of success beyond its endurance. *"Bonsoir, Madame,"* I said in turn to each French lady, "and I hope you enjoy your shrimps."

I walked through the wooden doors of the refectory and away to my room over the oceans of long slippery corridors that were empty and silent.

Here everything was waiting for me: the thick cotton eiderdown doubled over the end of the bed; the suitcases with their lids tipped up as I had left them, and, inside the neat pressed-together pile of bright materials that I had never worn, uneasy in their acclamation that their owner was aiming to be *en fête* after the long months of blue serge.

I felt quickly through the layers of soft things until I found among the hard objects at the bottom the photograph of my mother in its leather traveling frame. I put it on the bedside table and felt reassured; looking into the shadowy cardboard eyes I said with sudden certainty: I must get into bed, I am very tired after the journey. I'll build up the cushions behind my back and write straight off to Mother to tell her what fun it is to be here again. That I am being careful about my tummy. That nothing is really changed.

The light cotton curtains hung on widely spaced rings that did not slip easily over the bamboo curtain rod; I could not get the edges to meet. I could not dim the gilded evening that had just begun, that reflected its brilliance twice over into the green stillness of the garden pond outside my window. I could not muffle the sound of laughing and talking that drifted up from the strollers who wandered down to the sea wall to look at the sunset.

I knew very suddenly the full extent of my own aloneness; what it was going to be like after the inevitable deaths in the family; and that it would go on in this way until the more solitary moment of my own.

Tomorrow, I thought, I will try again. I will make a friend and try to lose myself in a group of jolly people who will accept me. At the moment I could do nothing about it, I was already in my nightgown and my face was smothered with cold cream.

I took up my pen and wrote:

Dearest Mother,
 It is wonderful to be here again. I feel as if I had never been away from it all, as if I was beginning my life all over again with a second chance. . . .

Now that we are beginning to regain consciousness there is the unspoken question hanging between us as to who will be the one to slither over the tiles, down the stairs to the kitchen door, and order the tea to be sent up. In the end, without speaking a word, it is I who, recalling Stephen's effort yesterday at the same time, slips out of bed and over the sun-baked floor.

The woman who looks after us is like a good-tempered marmoset. I have not yet been able to discover if she is the wife of the proprietor, or a servant; there are two of them exactly alike, dressed in the traditional black cotton; there is no distinguishing feature for foreigner to separate them.

When she puts the tray down on the table beside my bed, she does not go away, but pours out the first two cups; standing over us she watches for the effect of the strange brew. Rolling her blackcurrant eyes, she waits expectantly for us to leap in the air or utter weird sounds.

The English are always in bed, could well be her comment on our behavior. Yet they are not *too* productive.

When she dusts the dressing table, she plays like a child with the collection of little jars and bottles that I have brought with me. It has become a ritual joke, and each time I go through elaborate mime explaining: for the face, the neck, the eyelids. When I say, holding the bottle of dark oil, "*El sol,*" she laughs as at a mad woman, to think that I am trying to put something between myself and the heat that comes from the heart of God. "*La luna?*" she asked once wonderingly, but I could find no answer to this.

After the refreshing tea, we get off our thin chaff mattresses, leaving behind the crumpled sheets that have twisted to the size of large handkerchiefs. Our straw-plaited shoes, with the silver grains from the shallow sea embedded in their rope soles, have dried to the hardness of bricks; we do not think of changing them for another pair, our feet exposed and salted by the sea have become as toughly preserved as rawhide.

There are two hours left of the day. The sky, which is opalescent and glowing now, will deepen as the sun turns to a ball of fire; then it will suddenly slip down behind the mountains, everything slate-color in a matter of minutes.

The moment of adjustment, before the electric light of the island begins to work, is purgatorial and unrestful, but it is preferable to the weak wavering light that follows, under which it is possible to discern shapes but interpret nothing. We cannot read by it, we cannot guess the origins of what is on our plates.

"We must try and find that little ruined chapel, hermitage or whatever it is." Stephen, suddenly energetic, pores over the *Guide Bleu* that we have been lent by two French people in the hotel. *"Une petite mosquée,"* I remember the woman telling us, *"une atmosphère très rare."*

"It should certainly be easy to find," Stephen says. "The mountain lies exactly opposite the village church, the old girl said."

I am a little doubtful. It is a kind of breach of faith. When we come down on to the big verandah, we find the whole family sitting out, the women fanning themselves with newspapers, the men deep in talk—all but the boy Antonio, whose eyes are focused on the middle distance, out across the bay toward Barcelona, where he once spent a month: *"Très gaie, très moderne, beaucoup de musique."* He sighs nostalgically as he tries each evening to tune in on the wireless to the dance music from the mainland.

I ask him purposefully, hoping that he will be able to give us clearer directions: *"Vous connaissez la petite église dans la montagne?"*

But he is too far away, the leap too great: *"A oui, Madame."* He smiles politely. *"Petite église, très vieille, derrière la grande église, tres jolie. Bonne promenade."*

Breakfast next morning and no brown speckled egg on my plate; no fluted eggcup supported on a frail china base. All these things had been the prerogative of my youth; orders for supplements transmitted by my mother in her forceful French to the kitchen to spin out the austerities of conventual diet. Now I found only the white coffee bowl sprigged on the outside with blue flowers, settled on a thick plate with the addition of a sharp-pointed spoon and black-handled knife. There was a basket of sliced house bread and a large dish exposing four pats of waterlogged butter.

I was the first person at our table. I had been awakened very early by the sound of the martins under the eaves; then I had heard the clicking of rosary beads and the swishing of the black stiffened skirts of the nuns on their way to the six o'clock Mass. After that I had watched the face of my traveling clock too often and too eagerly for a signal to get up.

The French ladies arrived soon after me. Talking ecstatically, planning, dividing out their precious time so that they should extract the full benefit from their holiday. In a sudden rush of warmth, I imagined them inviting me to join them for a walk after luncheon; I could hear my own voice accepting, holding back my pleasure, so that it would not show too much. But they were already in conversation with the serving girl who poured out the bowls of coffee, ordering a picnic. With rugs and books and sun oil, they were going to the island for the day; they would return on the low tide in time for dinner.

It struck me suddenly, piercing the gentle warmth of the breakfast sun: suppose I am alone at this table for luncheon; suppose the young man, too, is going off for the day. The sweet milky coffee had a layer of yellow grease dotting its surface where the butter had melted; a crinkly skin was forming. I found that I was no longer able to swallow; the uncertainty had set going an acid tension. I lit a cigarette. Immediately I caught the eye of one of the ladies who were still eating and apologetically stubbed it out on my plate.

The young man came in just then. Pink-eyed, sleep-swollen, his thick hair standing up like a carpet brush. His clothes, too, looked as if he had tumbled straight out of bed after having slept in them.

"I can't wake up in the mornings here," he said in English to me, after he had greeted us all in halting French. "The air simply knocks me out at ten-thirty and I should probably sleep the clock round if someone didn't bang on my door at nine with the can of hot water."

He began to eat, slowly and systematically, and did not speak again until he asked, looking at my plate: "Could I have the remains of your butter if you don't want it?" Then with great skill he scraped the frail wisp onto the point of his steel knife and carried it over to his own plate.

"I'm going to sleep in the garden all day," he announced when he had finished his breakfast. We were now quietly inhaling the first cigarette of the day. "After yesterday on the rocks fishing, I'm unable to put one foot in front of the other."

I felt, returning to my room later, a sense of ease and relief. If I spoke to no one during the hours between meals, my silence could assume the significance of a self-imposed rest. He would be in the garden asleep, and I would be reading, writing my letters home, walking down by the sea wall or along the cliffs outside the stone fortress of the ancient monastery.

How lovely it was to be alive and walking up the village street at ten o'clock in the morning. I curved the soles of my feet luxuriously over the mottled cobbles, round as turkeys' eggs, that had been brought up from the seashore perhaps fifty years ago, and felt the heat of two hours' sun stored in them. The flowering hedges, pink-spiked daphne and trailing syringa, were buzzing with bees; the deep gloom from the ancient fig trees made pockets of underwater light along the roadside. In a cottage window there was still, as I had remembered it, a plant starred with white flowers. It filled the entire window, blotting out the light within the room; the darkness within and the lightness without equated the beliefs and fears of this fishing community. This plant was called Star of the Sea.

The woman in the bakery remembered me. As a young girl, before her marriage, she had been my nursemaid and sewed for my mother. *"Ah, mais vous êtes bien belle maintenant."* She embraced me, and ran her finger along the lid of my right eye.

I was glad to hear her say it; she was the first. I bought a curly loaf for my tea and went away smiling.

Down at the end of the village street there was a Calvary; a small hump of grass surmounted by a bare cross, it divided the two roads out of the peninsula. I took the left fork and walked above the level of the tarmac along a path lined with poplars. The tide was right out in the estuary, and the dry mud lay wrinkled by the complexity of dangerous currents that had seethed above it at high tide.

About a mile out of the village there was a house I was looking for, at the edge of the sea, just where the road wound inland a little before it reached the next village. This house was called Beausé; green-shuttered, with a fine iron scrolling on the balconies, it had deteriorated only in the superficial peeling and blistering of paint. It had been the *petit demesne* of some local family at the beginning of the last century. Now it had run to farmyard; the hens and ducks scratched on the balding grass at the front door that they used as often as the inhabitants; a wagonload of hay leaned easily against the lichened wall of the courtyard.

I stood looking through the iron railings and felt again the power of my mother's voice, so long ago, but never lost it seemed, absorbed and trapped forever in the stone and the high branches of the dark cypresses.

This had been the home of the second son of a well-known family (the elder brother a celebrated general who distinguished himself in the Crimea). At the age of forty he had retired from Paris with his collection of rare Chinese objects and original Louis XIV furniture. Quite suddenly he had married his cook, a girl from the village, but no bridge was ever made between their two quite happy and integrated lives; she kept to her kitchen and *potager*, and he to his library and drawing room. Children had been born to them without a hint of the aristocratic descent in their physique—brawny village boys whose papa was as remote to them as *Monsieur le Maire* or the village squire.

Often on the windy October days in my childhood, with the goldenrod dipping and sodden on its stems and the smell of charred gorse blowing across the wilder stretches between the sea, we had walked, my mother and I, past this house, sometimes catching a glimpse of an immaculate and Panama-hatted gentleman in his garden, who would bow courteously in recognition to the English visitors who stayed the seasons round. In the summer we would call at the house for strawberries that Madame sold; they were dark and sweet and long-stemmed, but larger than the wild berries that we sometimes found in the woods.

When Monsieur had died, Madame had pinned the ruin of an exquisite black Brussels' veil over her sunburned face; a gesture that was again without compromise, being a mark of perfect respect and a desire not to waste anything good.

Then she had gone about covering up the needle-point chairs and sofas with cellophane, and storing away the china and objects into glass-fronted wall cases. With her own death, the entire property had toppled, been gradually transposed by her eldest son into this tranquil and sleeping farmhouse—a farm however, to which it was still impossible to subject the chimney pots and the delicate ironwork of the windows and railings.

I shall never forget the sight of the big dark patches on the dry garden path; the village helpers had been drying the lettuce leaves, swinging them to and fro in rhythmic movements in the round wire cages. All day it had been heavy, the sky thick and opaque as pewter, descending nearer and nearer the earth, draining away the color from the sea and the rocks. These somber markings on the ground seemed then only symptomatic of the cloudburst that must surely follow.

The whole of that day I had spent indoors, going to the village only for the short space of time it took to clean my room. In the afternoon I had wandered along to the shuttered salon in an annex cut off from the rest of the house; here there was an upright piano, the same flared walnut case and crooked brass candlesticks that had always been there.

I lifted the lid and touched the slippery keys; there was a smell of dry dust and the powdering of long-dead moths; I ran my fingers up an octave expecting discordancies that would make me bang down the lid and go away, but it was in pitch. The discovery was exquisite and soothing. I started carefully working my way into the first movement of Beethoven's fourth piano concerto. I felt the power rising into my fingers and wrists; every note was under control, I could hear the line of the melody ahead of my own playing, leading me on, the high points of the phrases shaped themselves from my fingers effortlessly. When I had come to the end, I got up and went away back to my room. I lay for a long time on my bed hearing isolated phrases of the music and looking up at the ceiling, at the finely molded rosette in the middle that had become blurred by the frequent layers of whitewash. I thought, this is at last completion, an attainment of perfection that I had never hoped to hear from myself. The price I must pay is its secrecy. I think that I was happier then than I had ever been before in my life. This was my private harvest, and the knowledge of it was tempered with humility for the first time in all my thirty-five years.

Stephen Latterly and I had had tea together several times in succession. It had begun easily and without premeditation. Each time it came as a pleasant surprise and afterward I never feared for either its repetition or its cessation. When he said: "We must take a picnic over the estuary to Penguen when the tide's low enough," I thought the joy of anticipation is pleasure enough even if we never set foot over the corrugated ridges of sand.

At dinner that night the French ladies had added woolen jackets to their summer clothes; their mahogany skins now merged into the brackish fog that had blown into the house from the sea.

I said hopefully to Stephen Latterly, "This may

blow right away. I've known storms ripe and ready to burst blown to smithereens by a strong northeasterly wind." It was strange to think of the division of the elements against each other.

"We'll go down to the sea wall and watch the fight," he said. He, too, had added to his short-sleeved cotton shirt a purple cardigan knitted perhaps by some elderly relation who had been dreaming of a cathedral close.

Later, as we walked together down the broad flower path, up the little incline, made more durable by a wooden plank sunk into the earth, under the vaulted archway of plane trees and elms that separated the garden from the sea wall, I felt within myself the tired sweep of the past years that had led up to this afternoon of understanding in the music room. It was as if all my life had suddenly been explained away and that there would be no more to contend with but the minute pinpricks of existence.

Leaning together, on the points of our elbows, we looked out from the waist-high brick wall over the swiftly running tide that raced inland, reclaiming the sandy gullies between the rocks that marked out the path to the island. The sky was moving, shifting very slightly so that there was no longer the low mass of cloud that had hung over us all day. "It will win,"

Stephen said quite suddenly. "The wind, I mean. Look over there, beyond the headland, and you can see the break-up; the sky will be in shreds. There's the shadow of the moon."

It was very cold and I shuddered once or twice in spite of my plaid shawl. We were sitting back in an arbor of tamarisk on a low semicircular garden seat; the feathery plumes of the foliage and the delicate sprays of flowers were indistinguishable to the touch. Stephen took off his cardigan and, without speaking, hung it on my shoulders; for an instant his long fingers brushed against the skin of my neck. They were icy cold and he laughed at my involuntary shudder. "The finger of doom," he said. Yet it seemed to me that there was an underlying seriousness in his remark, something that reached out toward me further than anything he had ever said before.

"We'd better keep an eye on the time," I snapped more sharply than I intended, wishing only to reestablish the firm boundaries of our separate lives.

"Let's walk to the Point," he suggested. "I've left my watch in the room, but we're certain to hear the church clock chime the quarter hours."

Out on the short wind-bitten grass, climbing upward from the hollow of the abbey grounds, I soared, completely above the mesh of my anxieties. The sea wind swept into me, filling the arms and pockets of my clothes so that I was like a bird buoyed up with air sacks. "All through this hour," I shouted madly, "Lord be my guide," and then to Stephen: "I bet you don't know the words that go as the clock strikes the quarters!"

"And by Thy power," he shouted back, "No foot shall slide."

I was carried on by the release of the wind to say: "When I was about ten, I used to stand out here on the edge of the cliff and try to take off. I never thought that my inability to rise above the ground was due to anything less than my own lack of courage to take the chance and jump."

As we turned from the cliff's edge, now that the path began to wind inland, away from the dangerously crumbling precipice, the wind sighed and dropped a little. I wished that I had not said so much, talked so consistently about myself. Stephen took my hand from out of his cardigan pocket and held it in both his. "Hatty, I want to say something to you, now that the wind has dropped and we don't have to shout."

I reared up in embarrassment, ready to do anything to divert him. "Please don't. Anyway, this wind has made my ears sing. I'm as deaf as a post."

He went on, taking no heed of my excuses. "I heard you playing the piano this afternoon. I wasn't snooping, but I heard music coming from the salon when I was getting some drinking water from the pump and I came and looked through the slats of the shutters. I don't think I've heard anyone play like that before—the extraordinary clarity and bell-like tone—I didn't even know you had such a gift. Why do you teach music, when you can play like that?"

For a second I gathered to myself an advance guard of frustration and excuses that I would produce one by one to mislead him; then instead I found myself taking an enormous leap—almost with my eyes closed. "I hardly ever have time to practice these days; I teach children between the ages of twelve and sixteen; sometimes I go through a piece with the more advanced ones so that they can hear it in its completion." I thought that there would be a gluey kind of coziness in this admission, but it came away clean and whole. "I once had great hopes for myself. It was a freak talent; after I was fourteen I couldn't make any headway. Later I began to slip backward, I lost even the control to perform in front of an audience. That's all."

He was holding both my hands fast in his. "Poor Hatty," he said. "I think that's probably the first time

135

you've ever said that; the first time you haven't felt that someone else was to blame."

A tremendous relief washed over me. The moon was quite white and luminous, all the shreds of clouds blown away to nothing.

We walked back the way we had come, down into the hollow sheltered from the wind, hands linked together, yet I was aware of no staying pressure.

The stone walls of the outer fortress of the ancient foundation, nearly eight feet high, were mysterious and glittering with the encrustment of broken glass along the top. In a dream we came to the garden door let into the wall. It was locked—the narrow iron latch moved up and down like a dead twig that would not pull away from the main stem.

Stephen began to laugh aloud. "We shall have to fly now, right over the top of all that bristling glass."

But I was cleverer, knowing with long-accustomed hands and feet the small crevices and hollows in the wall that would lead us to the polished stone top of a grotto in the garden, from which it would be a straight drop onto the plushy grass.

Inside the grounds again, the thickets of privet and laurel rustled. The tall elms shrouded the moon. It was the sudden transposition from the openness and clarity of the cliffside that made me say woefully,

"I wish we'd had a watch. We'll never get anyone to hear us, and if one of the nuns come they'll be furious. . . ."

"You mean they'll eat us up because we've made a mistake over the time? Good God. . . ."

"It's always been like that," I snapped back. "Everyone who stays here knows that they lock up at half-past ten. They accept the rule as a small price to pay for peace. Les Colombes is also very much cheaper than any of the other *pensions*."

We were suddenly quarreling, and I wanted to pitch my annoyance against him to evoke a spark from the frenzy that was mounting within me.

"Shut up." The sharpness of his command shot to pieces the scaffolding of my resentments, leaving me empty and silent.

Up at the house all the doors were bolted and barred; we tapped lightly on the wood in case there should be some wandering sister on her way to bed who might hear. But no one came, and the lights in the windows were few and scattered—no one was within calling distance. By eleven o'clock the whole house was going to sleep.

I thought nostalgically about my bed. I had left it turned down, the plump eiderdown ready to pull up to my ears to keep out the cold night air.

Now the soft garden breeze stirred the long tails of hair off my neck; I hugged my shoulders more closely into the knitted material of Stephen's cardigan. Our feet on the graveled paths thundered in my ears like the galloping of horses' hoofs. I expected every moment to see a furious face at a window and hear the serpent's hiss of judgment. Yet no sound came from the gently breathing house, and nothing but the balmy night air disturbed the light curtains drawn loosely over every window.

"We'd better try that Moulin place," Stephen said. "They'll surely be able to give us a couple of rooms for the night; they didn't look very full when we had a drink there the other day. Anyway it will appeal to their sense of economics to rook us." He tapped the outside of his hip pocket, then, "Blast it," he said, "I must have left my notecase in my room with my watch."

I, too, had come without a bag. I hardly ever carried one, except when I went to the village specifically to shop.

We were going to be at a disadvantage, I knew, without ready money to bargain with; the wily hotel proprietors would be quick to see it. Eyebrows would rise as the price shot up; my family was well known in this village from many years' visiting; they would communicate their surprise at me without the mention of the word "scandal."

Because of the nebulous emotions that had been touched on earlier in the evening—scandal, love (both so closely allied in the geography of the heart)—I kept silent and, when we were once more over the wall and out on the cliff, I took the path that led into the peninsula running parallel with the village street until we could turn in at the market place to the baker's shop.

"Mimi will help us," I said. "She's the baker's wife and has known me for years; it's better than waking them up at the Moulin."

There was a brilliant light coming from the bakehouse beside the shop; the sound of clattering iron trays scuffling across wood. The heat rose through the barred air vents of the basement window, and there was the startling smell of freshly baked bread. I looked down through the window and saw the white-floured figures in their cloth caps and singlets moving silently from the long narrow tables to the waiting furnace.

I tapped gently on the darkened shop window, reassured by a gleam of light coming from a room at the back.

Mimi came to the door in her cotton overall that

she wore every day in the shop. Only the bundles of dark hair tied up into curling rags showed that she was preparing for bed.

"*Eh bien, vous prendrez la chambre a côté de la notre,*" she said managingly to me when I had explained, the same tone that she had so often used to me when I was a child and she thought it necessary to send me to bed early.

Then with her podgy fingers she thumped the upholstered seat of an upright chair in their living room, and she said that the mattress upstairs had lately been restuffed with feathers from the breast of Madame Puel's best geese.

It was white and cool in the small bedroom. The polished wood of the bedhead glowed like a darkly streaked cornelian. I sat tipping the sand out of my shoes into little silver heaps over the bare floor, thoughtfully and with great care.

When Stephen said: "You will have to marry me now, for better or for worse. I was going to ask you earlier this evening," I found I could reply, quite steadily, without the upsurge of any doubt or misgiving, that it would be for better or for worse, but that the worse was now far behind me.

Behind the village, dropping down below the parish church, we find a road cutting like a dry riverbed through the center of the island; in this pinkening light it is luminous as a pearl. A few stubbled fields slope away to the base of the hills. I see that there is a streak of path running into the dark of the conifers and pines. We follow it, and only when we have started the ascent do we find that it is broken and disconnected as a splintered bone.

"How do we know that this is the right mountain?" I say stupidly to Stephen. "At this distance any one of three might be the one immediately opposite the church."

"If this isn't the right one, we'll try another tomorrow." His reasonableness I find almost smug for a second. Yet I remember that once he said to me when I was in a state of great anxiety: "Nothing is very important, and few things are important at all." This shockproof philosophy I have liked in the past to wrap around myself; it could absorb the urgency of acute pain—and reduce the potency of hysterical joy. It is like a sense-killing drug that produces the kind of boredom that is incapable even of exterminating itself.

Now that we are deep into the trees, the light is green and pierced only here and there by the frail wisp of sky in the gaps. It is strange to find that it is so light and airy in these woods; there is no feeling of suffocation, or enclosure. Huge loose stones dislodge themselves from under our feet; we have to walk carefully, picking our way in and out. The path is overgrown; it loses itself in the curious detour of the ascent. What was clear and visible from the distance is now almost extinct and lost.

I realize that it is distance too that blackens things, as age obscures. The black woods seen from the beach are green and silvery beneath their branches. Yet it is not a young wood; the evergreen branches that are never stripped to nakedness bear the imprint of the skeleton in their silver arms; gray smooth lines mark out the extent of old age, even in the smallest sapling.

So we climb, panting with the strain of the steep ascent, yet buoyed up, the forces of gravity not operating, as if we could do nothing else but go on up.

Stephen is slightly ahead of me; I lose sight of him now and then as he picks up the path in and out of the trees. The hermit must have mortified himself by the irregularity of his ascent, never allowing the ease of a well-worn way. I think of him as he must have been in his mold-colored habit, staggering under the weight of a heavy water pot, rustling through the trees, then coming gratefully into the clear again.

As I draw level with Stephen, I say: "This isn't a much-trod path, is it? We must be the first for years."

He has found a resting place on a flat expanse of rock splashed with coarse yellow moss. I stretch out beside him and we look down through the tops of the trees at the distant loop of the bay. Smoking the Spanish cigarettes we have been reduced to, the straw-colored tobacco with the flavor of tea leaves and dried grass, I will myself to remember the exact flavor of pure Virginia tobacco.

"Perhaps everyone chooses his own path to the top," I say sleepily. On this sun-baked rock I could quite easily fall asleep, and give up the climb.

"The beginning and the end will be much the same. But come on." Stephen pulls me to my feet. "I can see the rot beginning to set in."

Still heavy with sleep, I mumble a slogan that would be unworthy even of Ted: "Equal chances with unequal potentialities." I would like to draw Stephen into a metaphysical argument, make him sit down again beside me on the lovely restful rock.

"What nonsense you talk," he says good-humoredly dragging me further away from the resting place.

"I'm really too old for all this adventure," I say,

for it is easy to be petty when one is thwarted in the heat. "If this is the wrong mountain, I shall roll down. I certainly shan't try another one tomorrow evening."

Now that he has prised me from the flat stone, Stephen has taken wings and streaked ahead. I can see the glitter of his white shirt disappearing through the green, putting out a hand here to pull himself forward on the silver arms of the pines that have the silken quality of young birches.

The witch's hat is narrowing to a point; but although we are aware of the sharpness of the outline, I am not in the least conscious of vertigo.

"This is good for the muscles in the thigh," Stephen shouts back to me. Unwillingly I have already started to follow him.

The idea of stones quarried at the base of the mountain, then piled into thick willow baskets, and carried by hand—for no beast would be able to overcome the rough stones of the track—is a feat made possibly only by a God-given desire for solitude and the contemplative life. Hermits who resort to caves make a natural compromise.

The way is so steep at times that I am bent almost double to keep going. I find that an extra sensitivity of the fingers makes me divine exactly the right stone on which to lever myself up without falling; my hands have become like febrile claws, the nails dust-rimmed and horny.

The trees are thinning a little, and there is a tiny plateau ahead. So, again it is an illusion that the mountain is pointed; only distance and the outline of the trees sharpen its tip.

"There," an extraordinary cry from Stephen. It trills like the pure note of a bird in this rarefied atmosphere that is so seldom disturbed by sounds other than the wind rushing through the treetops.

"There, look, a whitewashed mosque ahead."

I can see nothing from where I am. "Wait for me," I cry, clambering with all the energy I can muster until I reach his side.

Then I see it, the gleaming sugarhouse with a rounded dome mounted with a thin iron cross.

Here the fir trees are even paler and yellower; etiolated, in spite of their nearness to the sun, they are white gold. Tiny hedgerows of broom and rosemary run wild at our feet. The flatness is extraordinary, too; the plane we are standing on appears to have no boundaries, smudged into eternity.

What a perfectionist, and with what a talent for solitude, must have been the man who made his home here, with only the steep ascent as a lifeline to connect him with the outer world. In this place could be whittled down all experiences of the senses to such a sharp degree that the induced reactions of the world would assume the proportions of a nightmare. Self-conscious representations of man and beast could only be interpreted by such purity of mind as grotesque caricatures.

There is no door to the cell, only a dark mouth, soft and velvety against the crystalline whiteness of the washed brick. One must live in perpetual darkness, in order to experience the full purpose of the light.

Inside the round entrance we find ourselves in an outer chamber—a kind of empty limbo, where the birds have built and deserted their nests. As the retina of the eye becomes accustomed to the darkness, we notice that there is an inner sanctum from which radiates a curious power. Unseen tentacles reach out and draw us in. I feel suddenly that all the air and light is being pumped out of me, as if the act of breathing has become no longer a necessity. In this slate-colored vacuum it is like, I feel, St. Teresa of Avila's descriptions of her visions of hell: everything dim and colorless, yet completely distinguishable.

In the center of the farthest wall there is a plain wooden cross. No human Jesus with His arms outstretched to enfold His people, only the implement of torture as a terrible reminder. Golgotha without the last sad cries to bring the light into the sky once more.

From each of these wooden arms there hang garlands of withered flowers, *immortelles* as we call them, whose dry straw petals have never even held within them the sap of growing life. Attached to these, like lines of washing, there hang a collection of soiled infants' garments: tiny rotting boots, yellowing wool jackets and vests, satin bonnets that have gradually deteriorated to their original silkworm fibers.

By now our eyes have become completely accustomed to the dark; and the more we look about us, the more is revealed.

In roughly hewn niches on either side of the altar are stacked soldiers' and sailors' hats; crumpled letters and many faded photographs whose blurred sepia gives to the faces the quality of *revenants*. Rosary beads and medals hang from random nails on the wall. Everywhere there is an air of heavy and grievous entreaty, completely overshadowed and static, as if we stood in the shadow of a huge cliff from which we could never stir. All the agonies of supplication and despair lap around us.

"I can't stand this," I tell Stephen, as I push my way into the more bearable outer darkness. "We are experiencing all that the hermit ever had to put up with—and added to that the agonizing doubts and miseries of all the people who have come here to intercede through him."

Nothing is ever lost that is begun, no word spoken that can ever be broken down to uncoordinated syllables, no tear shed that will leave only a powdering of white salt. Everything must go on, and on, and on, repeating itself and gathering force for the ever that is still only the bright whiteness of eternity meditated on by mystics and recluses.

Stephen is still in the cell. He has not attempted to come out and join me. From the ledge I have found to lean against I watch his hands moving about from garment to garment, touching to carry in his memory the experience that I cannot face.

"I say," he calls out suddenly, "the walls are all covered with writing, had you noticed? I thought at first it was plaster cracks and fly dirt. Pity it's all in Spanish. Not even a word of French."

I cannot go back into the darkness to explore with him. Some kind of inarticulate fear compels me to turn away and take a cigarette out of my pocket. I look down through the trees toward the hidden bay, try to think about the descent.

When I turn back once more and look through the arched entrance, I am shocked to find that I am being observed by a pair of bright darting eyes: a brown bird sits silently in a nest packed into a hollow of the wall. It needs only the flapping of stiff wings in that enclosed space to complete the feeling of nightmare; it strengthens my resolve to stay in the open. If it was a nightingale and it sang in a faraway wood of a lost identity, I could forgive it the bat-brown wings and horny beak; it is the reality and the closeness that I cannot stand. I make this my pretext for not joining Stephen.

There is a plaque in the great Abbey of St. Albans, over an empty sarcophagus, that records the waywardness of a hermit. He destroyed the nightingales in the wood near his cell by fire, because they disturbed his meditations. Was it the fear of beauty, or the hindrance of love? The statement on the stone is mysterious and brief.

"This is what I make of it," Stephen calls out quite sharply, wishing me to go in and join him. "This cell has now become a kind of shrine since the hermit died or went away. It looks as if the people who have left their things expect in some way to be granted a request, and the bits of clothing are reminders of their personality. Perhaps they bargain and promise to return if they get what they want."

Now, I think, he is coming out and we shall be able to go away from all this unbearable suffering. I bend down to knot the cord of one of my shoes. But he does not come out into the light; he calls again, from the outer porch this time. His head is thrown back and his eyes are searching the walls.

"Just as I thought," he shouts. "These walls are covered with signatures and dates. Proof of the thanksgiving."

In curiosity, I risk the entrance again; it is after all only the outer edge, all the concentration of power and suffering seems to come from some indefinable place beyond the bare wooden arms of the cross. It reaches me still, yet diluted with the filtering sun and the resinous smell of pine needles it is made more bearable.

Now I can see clearly, all over the whitewashed walls of the interior, the spindly writing: *"Recuerdo, recuerdo"*; *Remember, remember*. Then the flourish of signatures, some as feeble as the legs of insects pinioned against the whiteness.

This holy man of the mountain has left nothing of himself; but on a rubbed brass plate are inscribed these words:

A EXP. DON PEDRO JUAN DE PEDRO
PUERTO SANTA EULALIA
ANNO 1358

Only that, and the magnetism of curiosity and myth that drew even such unsuspecting pilgrims as ourselves up the steep path, these centuries after his death.

I have overcome my feeling of fear and nausea: the impact of sanctity has now made me acutely sensitive, in the way that Stephen has been all along. I look curiously into what I could not face before.

"We ought to leave something of ours, don't you think?" Stephen searches in his pockets; but we have brought nothing with us, not even a handkerchief.

"Let's at least write our names," I say. "We can always come back another time."

Stephen is outside in the open now, and I have no fear to leave, or desire to join him. It is as if by having ceased to resist, I have released the atmosphere and pressure so that I can breathe freely.

Since we could find no pencil, Stephen comes in now with a sharp flint. He stands with his back to the shrine, searching the breadth of the wall for an empty space. Then, piercing the chalky surface, he scratches in neat letters our two names:

HARRIET AND STEPHEN LATTERLY

Watching him, I feel a curious sensation, as if my

eyes were peeled of scales; I feel receptive and calm, stronger than I have ever felt before.

He perfects his work, scratching a little here and there, touching up the points and loops that have been so difficult to form with the stone.

Suddenly, he turns to me with an amazed expression on his face. "Look, there," he says. "I can't believe my eyes. It's too fantastic that we should have come up here by such sheer accident."

I crane my neck backward to see where he is pointing; and it seems that the place is full of sunlight, as if by some curious coincidence the sun had just reached the entrance and now trained all its strength into the musty cell. I know in these seconds, before I find the place, that what I see I must never question, and that it will be important to me.

Then I read slowly, in a wavering Burgundian script that I have tried for so long to echo in my own writing, two names:

CYNTHIA MARY MILLER

JASPER LOMAX

and immediately below, in firmer strokes that might have been applied today:

Mon Amour Dura Après La Mort

—and the date of twenty-three years past.

A NOTE ON THE TYPE

Every Eye has been set in Caledonia, a type designed in the 1940s by the famed American typographer and book designer William Addison Dwiggins. The product of Dwiggins's wide-ranging efforts to create a type in the lineage of the Scotch romans of the early nineteenth century, Caledonia can claim a handful of types among its ancestors. Yet such was Caledonia's success that its mongrel heritage could not prevent it from taking its place among more thoroughbred types as one of the most popular book faces of the mid-twentieth century.

Design and composition by
Carl W. Scarbrough